The Human Hybrid

Odyssey

Forever Changed

A. McDonald, K. Witt,
and K. Jatta

Illustrations by K. Jatta

2nd edition 2023

ISBN:979-8-8690-9738-5

Village Life

Konni and Ey'lona were leisurely walking in the fields during the mid-morning hours. This is probably the best time to take a healthy walk in the fresh morning air. Hours before the day's high heat takes hold, and the ground beneath their feet gets too hot to walk barefooted.

The grass is almost perfect and reminiscent of a soft, plush carpet three inches deep. Walking through it is almost like walking on the clouds, with a hint of morning dew that hasn't entirely dried. Combine that with the sunny skies, with just a few white puffy clouds, and it is as perfect a day as one could hope for.

A leisurely walk in this part of the village territory is a rare treat. The everyday life in the village is a busy one, but it is also a bit mundane as every day seems to be an exact carbon copy of the last. From when the sun comes up to the time the sun goes down, everyone of working age has to perform. The village is quite large, yet very organized. The inhabitants of the village are not ordinary. They are "extra" ordinary.

The young couple was accompanied by their three-year-old son, Jvonn, the youngest in the village. He, too, is enjoying this lovely morning and its beauty, but just walking along is not his style. He is running, rolling, and hopping through the grass. He laughed and played tag with the grownups, who just slightly seemed to participate in his game, just enough to keep him laughing.

Occasionally, one of them will run after him and snatch him up into a bear hug to let him know they are paying him some attention. Then, place him back down to run around some more.

"I spend many nights wondering what the future may hold for our son," Ey'lona says.

"What do you mean by that?" asks Konni. "He will grow to be a great hunter like his father and his grandfather," he says.

Ey'lona replies, "I know that is the future you see for him, but that is such a narrow vision."

"When I was born, my parents raised me to be a hunter, which is what I trained to be. After their deaths, my grandfather ensured I stayed on that path, which worked out for me. Why wouldn't it work out for Jvonn?" said Konni.

"Hunting is a noble profession, but it has become the only profession around here," said Ey'lona. "You and I both were born in the village, and we know the many instances of yearning for more. Although we were both raised and trained to be hunters, that life was not as fulfilling as it is professed to be. The two of us always had each other, and we would steal away from the village every chance we got to explore each other and the outskirts of our land. We have always kept each other busy and entertained since childhood."

She continued, "Jvonn is the youngest of the tribe. There are no potential mates for him in the village. The older females are four and five years older than he, and they are all taken. There have been no other births since his, and no new births are expected. Our son will not have a wife if he stays in the village."

"I didn't think of it that way," said Konni. "I will need some time to consider what this will mean for his future."

It was then that Jvonn saw the butterfly. Like any child his age, his attention was diverted because he wanted to catch the butterfly. He scampered through the grass, arms outstretched, reaching as he ran behind the fleeing butterfly. The little insect would weave in very still in the bush as the unsuspecting herd grazed. Keeping low, they spread out to form a sort of semi-circle at a distance so as not to give away their presence.

The lions jumped out, and the deer began to run. They all tried to run in the same direction, and it was the wrong choice because the lions had already cut off that escape route. When they realized what was happening, the lions were taking some down.

Out of a herd of seventy or so deer, the lions took down twenty before the others could run for it. A significant part of the hunting plan is not to kill too many prey. This allows the deer to reproduce and grow their numbers for future hunts. Also, superstition has it that there is a giant elk (or deer) somewhere in the woods who will come for you if you kill too many of his herd. Many of the hunters laugh at the legend, but they still respect the idea.

The lions held tight to the captured prey as they continued to put up a fight. Once the fight was out of their hands, the hunters in human form moved in to take control of the deer, and the lions began to morph back into human form as well.

The hunters' ages range from ten to thirty years old. The youngsters do not catch anything until they are at least teenagers, but they can tag along to learn how the hunt is conducted and where the food comes from. The youngsters also participate in the after-catch activities like tying and carrying. Other tasks, like cutting up very large animals, are not for the young hunters.

The hunters were happy about the results of the plan, and they congratulated each other on a job well done. Then, they began the orderly process of gathering the catch, tying their legs, and loading them onto the transport with the other animal catches. This was a good hunting trip, and the hunting party was very proud of what they were bringing back home.

Bindi, one of the lead hunters, said, "Wonderful. This has been a very productive trip. Let's wrap it up so we can head back home."

The lead hunters summoned all the others to begin securing the catches for transport. The hunt was over for this trip, and it was time to pack up and head home.

Back at the Village

Back at the village, as the hunters were returning from their day out, the catch was bountiful, and the village could eat at least two weeks off the meat. There were bison, antelope, many rabbits, hogs, turkeys, ducks, and zebras. Larger prey is usually cut up in the field and brought back in large pieces. Larger prey, rarely pursued, would be rhinos, elephants, hippos, and large buffalo. Most of this bounty would come in whole, except the bison. There were also more than two dozen wild boar.

One would think that the sight of such a sizable haul would excite the people, but this was a regular ritual. The hunters go out early one morning, then return after several days when their hands are full, and their energy levels are not. The hunters always come through. The village never goes hungry.

Bindi and his hunting counterpart, Nosoo, divided up the job of coordinating the offloading of the cargo while the rest of the hunting party headed for their homes and families.

The village itself is not so magnificent as it is cozy. Its looks from the outside are not so glorious that anyone would clamor to gain access to it, but it has a certain appeal. Nothing about its appearance says that living there is easy or that life there is a luxury. Yet the sense of responsibility and the family atmosphere makes it so inviting.

The land the village sits on is as level as it could be, considering the makeup of the terrain. Rolling hills, the occasional bolder, and smaller pesky plant life present a challenge. Clearing an area to fashion a home requires some creative planning and insights, not to mention the long tree roots extending so far from the giant trees that provide shade. There are no machines or heavy equipment like there were hundreds of years ago, before the near decimation of the human race. Building anything worth having must be done by hand and with the few tools they can fashion.

Temperatures are optimal at a steady 80 degrees Fahrenheit, without the humidity, and a cool breeze blows, almost on queue. Rain comes when it is needed, and it does not overwhelm the area. No huge downfalls that flood the plains or wash away the crops. Rivers remain at just the proper levels and do not overflow their banks in this area. After all, at one point in time, this land was lovingly called 'Paradise' because of all the favorable amenities it offered.

The homes are made of wood and straw. Windows are merely openings on the outside of the house, with a cloth on the inside that provides privacy. The entrance to each is a longer piece of cloth hung from the top of the doorway, and entry to any home is respected by knocking on the wooden frame closest to the door and calling the name of the person you are seeking. The roof is fashioned from sticks, leaves, straw, and mud. They keep the rain out very well.

Every family unit has a den, some larger than others, but dens can be enlarged as the families grow. If the family grows large, they may be required to move their den to an area that can accommodate the size they need. Families can grow by the birth of children or addition by marriage. When a marriage occurs, the female moves in with the male's family. Either way, more space will be required. Unfortunately, in such a small village, almost everyone is related to each other over time, and that brings about its own set of problems.

Several generations of a family can reside in a family unit simultaneously. This is the custom. The current record is five generations, but four is more common. The oldest male, who is still able-bodied, is considered the 'Patriarch' of the family and speaks for them as well. When this male can no longer hunt and protect the family, his oldest male son, a hunter, becomes the family patriarch. Like all families throughout time, disagreements arise and there become challenges to the patriarch designations. These charges are settled in The Village Chamber.

The Village Chamber is very similar to our 'Court of Law' because everyone involved gets to lay out their grievance before a group of randomly chosen peers. The big difference is that no one goes to jail when it is over. The decision of the chamber is unimpeachable. Once it is handed down, there will be no more protests.

***

Konni, Ey'lona, and Jvonn returned to the village just as the hunters entered. Konni tells Jvonn to go to their den so he and Ey'lona can get started doing their part in bringing in the hunters' catch. He also reminds Jvonn to stay out of the way of the villagers because they will all be busy working hard to prepare and store the food.

The trio takes off in different directions. Ey'lona walks toward the Great Hall. Konni walks briskly towards the Center Square. Jvonn scampers off toward their home on the Northeast side of the village.

Their home is almost 300 yards from the center of the village. It is not in the shadiest part of the village, but when it was built, an overhang was added to the front to make enough of a shaded area where several people could sit and avoid the sun for much of the day. This is not the only dwelling with an overhang, but their overhang was a little more significant than most. This was to accommodate the village elders, who sometimes would gather at the house to converse with Konni's grandfather.

Currently, the dwelling is just twenty feet wide and thirty feet deep. Two areas are separated, with walls, to create bedrooms for privacy. There is one large area that would be considered the shared family room. This area has seating, tables, and animal skin throw rugs. These items are considered furniture and were handmade by people in the village. Many villagers have unique skills that help keep their lifestyle going.

There are no lights because there is no electricity. There are no torches or lanterns either. Fire is used sparingly to cook meat or heat water. These people live in the sticks with no conveniences. Light comes from the sun, the moon, and the stars, and some nights are pitch black. It is a good thing that they have the eyes of cats and can see better than regular humans in the dark.

When Jvonn arrives home, he is met by his great-grandfather sitting out in front of the house. He immediately goes to his side and, before he sits down, greets his 'GG Pa' with a smile and a look into his eyes. This is the greeting of love and respect.

GG Pa was a tall and powerful-looking man. he stood over six feet tall and weighed over 250 pounds, mostly muscle. his thick white hair had grown down just below his shoulders. His garments were unlike anyone else in the village, and no one had ever tried to duplicate them. He wore armbands on his forearms and a specially made pair of boot-like sandals. Around his neck was a genuinely elaborate and intricate-looking necklace paired with an amulet embedded in his forehead. His eyes were piercing, as if he looked straight through people and objects. He had a commanding presence wherever he went and spoke with authority. Even his waistband looked notable and distinct. And GG Pa was 80 years old.

"Good afternoon, GG Pa," he says. "May I sit?"

His GG Pa motions to his left side to approve Jvonn's request to sit.

After Jvonn sits down on the ground, he begins to ask the questions on the minds of all who are so young. Why, why, why? Although some may find these questions annoying or exasperating, GG Pa, in his great wisdom, knows that this is how he gets to pass on the lessons he has learned in life to someone more than willing to listen.

Jvonn begins to ask his questions:

When will I be old enough to help?

GG Pa says, "In a few more years, once you have grown more muscles."

Jvonn says, "Where do they find all those animals they bring back?"

GG Pa replies, "There are many, many animals out in the vast wilderness," as he waves his arm towards the open lands. "These other animals are of all sizes and shapes. When you go out hunting, you will see how great the animal kingdom is."

Jvonn asks, "When will I learn how to hunt?"

GG Pa responds, "It will be a few years, but time will go by fast. You will be a great hunter like your father and his father before him."

"How can I be like my grandfather if I never met him?" Jvonn asks.

"You already have many of his manners," says GG Pa, "These things are naturally inherited through the family, and as time progresses, additional family traits will emerge."

A Light in the Western Sky

Dinner at The Great Hall is an everyday occurrence. All meals are served at the Great Hall, and everyone within the village is welcome to participate in any meal. One caveat is that you may be asked to help serve the meal or do another job when entering the hall. And the absolute custom is that you will comply.

Many villagers are hard at work preparing the hall for the incoming haul of meat that the hunters have captured. Large vats are being filled with water in one area as the water "team" brings in the buckets, one behind the next. Salt is also being piled up next to each vat because salt is still the village's best preservative. And then there are the tunnels.

The tunnels are huge holes dug down at least fifty feet. The villagers have found that the temperature in the tunnels is a constant 30 to 35 degrees, which helps keep the meat from spoiling quickly. The holes are round and five feet across on all sides. Platforms, secured by ropes, hold the barrels filled with meat lowered into the tunnels. Several platforms can sit on each other, but the barrel closest to the top must be 20 feet from the surface. This makes it hard for anyone who is not supposed to be removing food to access it quickly, and that's where the temperatures remain steady.

Outside the hall, a large group has gathered with knives and machete-like tools to dismantle the larger animals. The larger the animal, the longer it will stay fresh in the tunnels. It probably has to do with the fact that the enormous animals have always had to survive in the elements or have more substance in their bodies. The smaller animals begin to rot faster, so they are the first items on the menu after storing the bounty.

The bounty is separated in the order in which they will be eaten. The meat on this evening's menu is sent directly to the fire pit area. The meat that lasts longest and will be eaten nearer the end of the bounty running out is moved deep into the cold storage area. Everything in between is placed in the most appropriate cold storage area that best suits their flesh.

There are no particular or reserved seating areas for the villagers, but some tend to sit in the same general area each evening. Especially the 'Old Timers.' These are the wiser leaders of the village who grew up together and have been close allies and friends for decades. They tend to like talking and telling old stories together. Memories of the "Good Old Days" are always welcome conversation. Sometimes, they would sit and reminisce about other members of their tribe who had already passed on. They would talk about the good times and the challenges that they made it through. It was all their hard work that made the current village possible.

Once the dinner has been eaten and the utensils are cleared from the surfaces, the group is called to order by the 'Village Scribe.' This individual is usually elected for their ability to listen and to speak. The representative will receive information from many people in and outside the village. Information from outside of the village is extremely rare. Then, they must pass the information on to the rest of the village, including any updates. The job is not one of power. It is an administrative function to keep everyone in the know.

This evening, the scribe will first thank the gods and the hunters for the wonderful bounty brought into the village. After this, any business received from the 'Kingdom of Imbube' is relayed. The Kingdom of Imbube is the seat of the King to whom the village is subject, even though most villagers had never laid eyes on the actual kingdom.

The village was founded, built, and settled forty years ago when the semi-hybrids did not entirely trust many hybrids. It was more politics and the struggle for power than anything else. At the time, fifteen families decided to leave the confines of the kingdom to live on their own, but they would always be loyal to the Imbube kingdom.

After settling in their new village, their lives were forever changed for the better. The nearby water streams were perfect for drinking. The area soil was ideal for growing their few crops. There were several fruit trees in the area. And most of all, there was plenty of open space for their village to grow for the many years to come. The ocean was pretty close, but it was a long walk. The people used an old method to harvest salt from the sea and then transport the salt back to the village.

There is no relay from the kingdom this month, and no news is good news, right?

Next is the business of the village. A couple in the village, Bindi and Yani, are planning to marry, and everyone is given notice of the day and time. Although there are no clocks, time is represented by the sun's position relative to the constructs placed outside the village by the ancestors. The wedding will take place eleven days from today when the sun is over the trees of the Southwest. That would be about three o'clock in our day.

One of the villagers yells, "Do they have to get married, or do they want to get married?" And many in the hall laugh loudly because they find it funny.

Bindi stood up quickly to say, "We must get married because we want to get married."

There is more laughter.

The Scribe asked if anyone had anything else to share before the meeting and meal were concluded. Now, the entertainment can begin. Steins of ale are brought in and passed around as someone starts singing a song. Slowly, others join in until almost the whole hall is singing along. This is a folksy tune that was passed down through the years. It is a song that gets into your head and makes you think about your place in the world and your destiny.

Once that song is complete, a group of three gets up on the podium and starts singing a song they have created and practiced. It is a good song, and the audience is entertained. More acts like this follow for over an hour before the villagers pour out of the Great Hall. Most villagers go toward their homes, but others will still gather to sit in circles and have debates and discussions. This is mainly a group of men who want to express their opinions on the events of concern.

Konni is participating in these discussions and decides to ask a pointed question. "For many years, this village expanded and improved over time, but for the last ten years, we have stagnated and developed a rut." He continued, "We hunt and grow food on a schedule. We eat and socialize on a schedule. We keep to the boundaries of the village. Is this all the future we have to offer to our children?"

"My son is the youngest child in the village. He is years younger than the next child and there have been no other births since his. What future does he have if we, as a village, do not expand outside our comfort zone? Where will he find a mate? How will my family line continue?"

At that moment, one man jumps up in excitement to say, "Look. Over there in the sky." Pointing off in a Westward direction.

When the group looked up and off to the Northwest, there was a light. The light was more like a glow, with a greenish-yellow hue. The light looked sort of weird above the treetops of the dense forest. And because it was so far away, it seemed a bit dull but very unnatural. This was not a fire nor a reflection of the moon because they could see the full moon high in the night sky.

The moon brings its own eeriness and mystery. A full moon makes the forest's trees look almost alive while the miles-long stretches of tall grass appear to move. The moon's glow seems to create the wisps of fog that float scarily just feet off the ground. A full moon makes for an exciting night.

Another villager mentions that she and her family had seen the same light the previous evening. It was late, and they were home preparing for bed. By morning, she had forgotten all about it.

Whatever was causing the light needed to be examined. This was an anomaly in the region, and it required an immediate inspection. The village would send a delegation to the area first thing in the morning. They needed to find the underlying cause of this quickly.

The group continued their discussions while simultaneously keeping eyes on the mysterious glow.

Kima, one of the Elders, said, "This issue has been raised in smaller consults, and the Council is diligently working to develop a plan."

Konni says, "The only solution is to find another lion tribe and work with them to extend our bloodlines. Theirs and ours."

GG Pa says, "That would be the simple solution, but things are a bit more complicated than that. Not all lion tribes are compatible with our bloodline."

"What is that supposed to mean?" says Konni.

Suddenly, a second light, much smaller, appeared. This second light began to glow and then started to grow. This second light was a much more familiar one. It was a fire. It also looked to be an exceptionally long distance from the village but just a short distance from the strange glow that was first spotted.

The fire looked to be just about where the Hyenas had a settlement. The hyenas and the lions are not the best of friends. In fact, they barely tolerate each other. However, they felt something was burning, and judging by the size of the fire, something was not right.

A Journey to the East

When the sun rose, and after breakfast, a group was selected to take the long walk and represent the village. The group was all male only because the females were responsible for much of the village arrangements. This way, the village could continue functioning while the males were away. Additionally, there were just a few of them making the trip.

They only packed or carried a little since they could morph into lions and hunt their food. Also, they knew there were several small and one large bodies of water along the way. Blankets to sleep on were a necessity, so everyone carried their own. The walk would be long, and the environment would not be a cakewalk. There would be challenges along the way. They were taking the shortest route rather than the easiest route. The easier route would add a couple of days to the trip, and they just wanted to see what was happening out in the distance and get back home to their daily lives.

The conversation was light and pleasant when the trek began as they walked through the grass with the occasional brush. When they reached the forest, the conversations had to stop because their attention had to be directed toward the unknowns that could jump out at any turn. No matter their form, a snake bite can be painful, if not deadly.

Vimal, a strong and respected hunter, told the group, "We will walk briskly, keeping good watch for dangerous or risky situations. This is an intelligence gathering, which should not include injuries."

***

The group, led by Bindi, had traveled almost thirty miles to satisfy their curiosity. Something was burning in that direction, and they knew that the Mafisi tribe had a large settlement. Based on the proximity of the smoke, it was looking more and more like it was coming from their settlement.

The Mafisi tribe are a fierce people, hyena people, with a penchant for distrust. They are very suspicious of those who come through their area, and many have found that their hospitality begins at the tip of a spear or with a noose around the neck. They are very protective of their land and their people. Tradition dictates that they intermarry amongst their people. No

27

outsiders. Such a tradition has led to the most inbred group of hybrids ever. Ironically, the tradition meant to "protect" the bloodline is the biggest threat to wiping it out.

As is the custom, when the hunting group arrived at the edge of the settlement, the tribal call of the Mafisi people was given as an alert that they were entering the Mafisi territory. The hunting group would also stop and await an escort to the center of the settlement. The escort would usually take just a minute or two, but it had been five minutes, and still no sign of the escort. The group gave the tribal call again, this time as loud as they could—still no sign of the escort after three minutes. Also, the area seemed to be much quieter than what they remembered.

There was no sign of life except several large birds circling overhead. They were not predators or scavengers, but they were pretty big. More like hawks. They were flying in circles and looking down.

Bindi said, "I don't like the way this feels. First, it is much too quiet for Hyenas, and second, the weird birds are flying around."

The group moved closer to the settlement area slowly and deliberately, looking around carefully as they went.

Suddenly, they noticed a body halfway on and halfway off the trail. They rushed over to see what was wrong. The body was unmoving, and one arm was missing. It appeared to have been ripped off. This person was dead. The group looked at each other, mystified and terrified. They were all thinking the same thing, "What could have happened here?" The direction of the body suggested that this person was probably running away from the general direction of the village before they were killed.

Vimal whispered, "Be very quiet and be very prepared."

Now, they moved forward with even more caution, almost tippy toeing their way forward so they wouldn't alert an adversary if the adversary were still in the area. The group also took a defensive posture, just in case. They did not want to be surprised; if someone or something jumped out, they wanted to be ready for action. They spread out to keep a three-foot distance between them, and the two in the back kept their "heads on a swivel" to guard against anyone, or anything, from coming up from behind.

They moved closer, and a second body was on the ground, badly damaged. A third body was in some brush, but it had been decapitated, and it too was severely damaged. After that, the view was several dead bodies scattered around, but there were also trails of blood leading away from the settlement. Based on the way it looked and because only about nine or so partial bodies lay around, the number of unaccounted souls is estimated to be over two hundred.

The group made their way closer to the middle of the settlement, passing several more dead as they went. Once at the center of "town," the scene was surreal. Signs of a struggle were evident and there was no doubt that the Mafisi were outmatched. Blood splattered and smeared on everything. The smoke seen from a distance resulted from several homes that burned, but not all were torched. All was quiet, and nothing moved. They put out as many of the small fires they came across as they wandered through the settlement. Some fires had already burned themselves out and were smoldering.

What happened here? Why were they attacked? Who could have done this? And it looked as if they were caught entirely by surprise. Weapons were still in their resting places, and the drag marks indicated that the inhabitants were dragged out of their homes. Some signs indicated that the inhabitants struggled, but it was useless. This was a slaughter.

The group looked around for quite a while and found no survivors; they were able to locate the food storage and pulled out some things to eat. They were famished from the long walk and the crazy situation. There was little food left, mainly fruits and vegetables. There is no sign of meat, which is strange. This tribe thrived on meat, so having a meatless storage barn is bizarre. However, there were signs of meat having been in the storage barn very recently, but someone took it all.

After eating a host of fruits and vegetables and drinking refreshingly cool water, the group took one more tour of the settlement. They walked in and out of several dwellings a little deeper in, but still, no one was there. In some, there were signs of struggle, while some had no signs of struggle at all. Still, other dwellings had outside damage, punctuated by blood stains. There was no explanation that they could think of, and the consensus was to head home quickly and report what they had found.

Bindi said, "We have to get back home and warn our people. Whatever happened here cannot be allowed to happen in our village."

"The way I see it, they were taken by surprise late last night and hit hard and fast. I don't think I can ever sleep again," said Vimal

The group pulled themselves together, accounted for everyone, and made their way out of the settlement. They made sure to fill up their water and take a few rations to help them on their journey home. As they walked back out of the territory, again passing all the horrible sights they saw on the way in, they were terrified. Whatever had wiped out this settlement could return before they got out. Their walk became a little more hurried.

Overhead, the large birds were no longer circling in the sky but perched high in a tree. They were sitting there, looking down. Unmoving, except for the occasional blink of their eyes.

"Those birds are really making me nervous. It's like they know something that we don't," said Vimal.

Getting Back Home

After the Imbube left the area, a Mafisi hunting party, away for days, returned to the settlement to see all the devastation and destruction. They wailed at the loss of their families and friends. Each hunter ran toward their own home to check on their loved ones, only to find no one. All that was left for them to see was blood and destruction.

Looking all around, inside, and out, there were no signs of life. No children were playing. No meals were being prepared. The halls were empty, and the homes were vacant. There was nothing left of the settlement other than the structures.

As the initial shock began to wear off, they expanded their search. They walked in the same direction the Imbube group used and saw the bodies over in that direction. They were able to identify all the bodies, including the one that was decapitated. All this just caused them to hurt more and yell out in pain.

Since the group from Imbube was there on a humanitarian visit, they left several tracks to indicate that they had been there. The hunting party looks at these tracks as evidence of the atrocity that happened in their village. However, some of the other hunters found tracks leading in a different direction, and these tracks were substantial paw prints, unlike the other footprints. They also realized that the blood trails followed the same path as the paw prints and not the footprints. The culprits were animals, not humans.

***

When the group finally arrived home, they were filled with excitement and anxiety from what they saw at the Mafisi settlement. Although it was a long and strenuous walk through the elements and the terrain was not exactly favorable, the group felt it necessary to relay the news they had seen.

In the middle of the village is a vast horn system, with sounds going out in four directions. This horn system is used to call the village to attention. Based on the number of sounds emitted, the villagers will react to it.

Bindi went to the horn and blew into the system three times in three-second intervals. Then he paused for ten seconds before repeating this cadence. Again, after ten seconds, he blew into the horns a third time. Before he had finished the third cadence, many villagers were already moving quickly to The Great Hall. Young and old alike were heading briskly toward the hall, asking each other if they knew what was happening.

All the villagers hustled to The Great Hall as quickly as they could. Young and old alike made their way into the hall and to their pre-arranged seating areas. Jvonn and his family sat to the left, just a few feet from the group that would make the presentation. GG Pa sat in a separate area on the presentation stage. This area was reserved for the Village Elders whose wisdom and leadership had founded and kept this village thriving for over 50 years.

Once all the villagers had arrived, Bindi began his oration to describe the past week's events and what the group had discovered.

He began by telling them how they made the journey to the West on the suggestion of the Village Council, right after the large plume of smoke was seen in the distance. He described the journey and how far they had to travel before they realized where the smoke was coming from, but not the cause of the smoke. Bindi went on to describe the moment the group realized that the smoke was coming from The Mafisi

Settlement, and they were not keen on advancing further, but they did so anyway. He described how no one answered his calls to the settlement's residents.

Then he began to describe the gory details of the mutilated and decapitated bodies that lay in the dirt as they inched closer to the living area of the settlement, how they noticed bloodstains on the side of living areas and broken tools on the grounds. He also spoke of how they could see a trail of drag marks, with bloodstains, trailing off to the North. It looked like the inhabitants were caught off guard and never stood a chance. No one had survived.

Whatever happened in the settlement, it was devastating.

The villagers sat in awe at the description of the settlement's condition when the group arrived. One person raised their hand to ask, "There were no survivors in the village?" Bindi responded, "not one."

Another person asked, "Do you know, or have a good guess, what happened?"

He said, "No, I have no idea, but large animal tracks were leading away from the settlement."

There was an uneasy silence for about five seconds before one of the Elders, Maneek, leaned over to the other Elders and said, "I don't want to jump to a conclusion, but this sounds like the work of Tagati."

One of the villagers asks excitedly, "Who or what is Tagati?"

The Story of the Wolves

GG Pa begins, "When I was just a young boy of 10 years or so, there was a man who was an adviser to the king. His name was Umholi. He was a lion hybrid and the leader of the Spiritual Resources.

One day, several warriors who had been out on patrol returned to the Royal Grounds in a frantic state because many of the soldiers who had gone out with them died after drinking from a familiar water source just a few miles away. Some warriors who had made it back also drank the same water, but it must not have been enough to kill them immediately. They became ill and dehydrated, some more than others, but they did not die.

An emergency meeting of The King's Cabinet was called. Umholi was part of that Cabinet. The group of leaders debated the pros and cons of each course of action presented but could not form a consensus on what to do. They could not even agree on what may have been the reason for the unknown illness that struck the warriors.

One of the theories was that an enemy of the Kingdom had poisoned the water to kill as many of the King's warriors as possible to weaken their defenses. A few Cabinet members subscribed to this theory and argued for retaliation. Umholi argued loudest and most vigorously. He even decided that the enemy that had done this evil deed was the Tribe of the Mafisi—the Hyenas.

The lions and the hyenas had not been getting along for all the years since the Great Punishment. Not that they blamed each other for the situation everyone was in, but because, naturally, each group wanted to be the dominant force. The lions didn't want the hyenas in charge, and the hyenas didn't want to take orders from the lions, so they met secretly to plot an overthrow of the king. This caused a lot of strife in the land and fighting among the groups; however, none of the encounters resulted in death.

The last time there was a severe disagreement, the two sides were close to an all-out battle, but cooler heads prevailed. An agreement was struck to prevent any bloodshed by putting distance between the two groups. A property line was established by landmarks that kept the two groups at a distance of at least 50 miles.

Although the hyenas established their own colony, it was still not to be, in any way, assumed to be a kingdom. Thus, the designation of "settlement" was attached to the areas.

The King wanted more information on what had caused this illness and whatever protections could be gathered to prevent the rest of the Kingdom from falling victim to the disease. Especially since the stream was one of the water sources for the Kingdom and the immediate surrounding area. A couple of thousands of people were dependent on water in the area.

The King assigned the diplomat to arrange a meeting with the Ingwe Tribal Leaders to discuss the illness affecting the water. This was to go out as an urgent request of the utmost importance. A messenger was dispatched immediately.

The King assigned the counselor to have his underlings meet with the kingdom's subjects in groups to deliver the news of the illness, where it was discovered, and to avoid the water source known to have it. The counselors should also assure the people that The King and his council were hard at work addressing the threat and working to neutralize it.

The King assigned Umholi to create an antidote to the sickness because Umholi used chemicals and formulas as part of his spiritual healing. The antidote would be used in case the illness struck anyone else. Still, hopes were that the antidote could be administered to the populace to protect everyone from falling victim to the disease.

The King assigned his detective chief to send spies into the communities to gossip or talk about the illness and its origins. Perhaps someone in the kingdom already knows where this illness came from.

Time was passing, and Umholi grew more anxious. His work to create an antidote was not producing the results he wanted or expected. Instead of focusing on correcting his shortcomings, he grew angry with his dislike of the hyenas until it burned in his eyes. He insisted that the hyenas would pay for this, although he had no proof that they were the source of the illness or that it was meant to bring down the lion kingdom.

The messenger was expected to return after ten days, but on the fifteenth day, he was not back. The council was called to gather again.

The debate began immediately with a conclusion that the hyenas had killed the messenger and disregarded the invitation. The council was pushing for a confrontation. A battle. A war. However, the King was not the King because he listened to fools. The King pushed back with full force. The idea of confrontation was snuffed out. The Kingdom would send a small delegation to follow up on the messenger and speak with the Mafisi Tribe.

Umholi stormed out of the council meeting and returned to his home, muttering incomprehensibly all the way back. The anger in his eyes was only second to the anger in his heart. He knew the hyenas were responsible and would not let them get away with this deed. He would make them pay. He would make them pay dearly.

Umholi remembered an old witch doctor who lived in The Cave of Inyoka. He had been banished from the Kingdom many years ago for practicing Black Magic, and Umholi thought he would be the perfect person to help him because it was something the king would not like. And if the king didn't like it, the witch doctor would love it.

Umholi snuck out of the kingdom under cover of darkness and began a two-day trek to the cave. He had taken a ration of food and water to help him make the long and dangerous journey. His determination and anger overwhelmed his sense of self-preservation.

When Umholi arrived at the rumored location, there was nothing but a dark cave. There was ivy along the walls and the opening, and a lot of brush led up to the opening. If he did not know that there was supposed to be an opening to the cave, he would never have seen it behind all the growth. However, there was no sign of anyone or anything.

He stepped closer to the mouth of the cave and yelled, "Hello?" No answer.

He stepped inside, and to his surprise, after just a few yards, the small dark opening blossomed into a massively glorious, almost welcoming, chamber. Except for the gruesome-looking horrors carved into the cave's walls and ceiling, it might make a lovely reception hall. There was plenty of room on all sides, and natural light shone from above.

Umholi could slightly make out the sound of rustling as it echoed off the cave walls. It was a faint sound at first, but then the volume grew louder. Umholi tensed up, not knowing what to expect, and he was right. Before he could take a step back, a giant Boa Constrictor quickly wrapped itself around him. He didn't squeeze. He just kept him immobile. Then the face of the witch doctor appeared before him, absent a body. It was just floating before him.

The dis-embodied head seemed to glow as it laughed in his face before demanding to know why he had come into his lair uninvited and disturbed him.

Three giant cobras raised their heads and stood at Umholi's height, eyeing him from three feet away. The cobras were more prominent than any he had ever seen. They looked more like those giant anacondas with bodies as round as a tree trunk and heads as big as a human torso. Just looking at the three cobras loosened his bowels, but not so much as to allow anything to escape.

Umholi was terrified now and wondered if this was such a great idea. This is not the way he thought this would go down. Then again, he had no idea how this would go down. He didn't think this through. Maybe he could have counted to ten and taken a deep breath before he decided to come here. Too late now.

The floating head said, once again, "Why have you disturbed me?"

Umholi stuttered, "I need your help."

"You need my help," the head laughed. "I don't help. I abuse. Why would you think I would help you?"

Umholi said, "Because it would bring down the king."

The head said, "Bring him to me." And the boa began slithering into the cave's darkness, still holding Umholi. The cobras escorted them as well.

Umholi was taken deep into the cave. They passed many corridors and made several turns, both left and right. The cave was a virtual maze of darkness, yet these snakes moved through it with complete confidence that they knew where they were going.

The cave drew very dark before he began to see a sliver of light again. When they exited the cave, Umholi saw the Witch Doctor sitting on a rock. The rock resembled a throne with a footrest in front of it. On either side were two small rock chairs, less nice looking. The makeshift thrones sat in the middle of four trees that formed a semi-circle behind them. The trees were reminiscent of giant security guards. Unfortunately, they had no leaves because this was the planet's dark side, and there was no sunlight over there, just moonlight, and a quarter of the time, there was no light from the moon either.

There is no grass, weeds, or other green plant life, just the skeletons of what used to be—many dead-looking shrubs without leaves. Just four feet of trunks and stems and many, many thorns. These barren shrubs filled in the spaces between the trees in the semi-circle. The density of the shrubbery made it impossible for anyone to move between them. They formed a proverbial wall, but not enough to stop a snake.

The witch doctor, Tagati, was slim and dark brown, all except his head. His dreadlocks were long and straight. He wore several necklaces, each made of different stones and minerals. Each had its mystical reasoning to magnify any of the powers he possessed. His head was adorned with a twelve-foot viper, and his face was painted to match the colors of the viper. This made his head look like a continuation of the viper, as Tagati considered himself.

Tagati told the boa to release Umholi. As the boa released him, the snake slithered away into the darkness.

"Come closer, "Tagati said, "let me hear this proposal of yours."

Umholi stepped up and began to tell Tagati how the king would not confront the hyenas while the people were dying of the poison that was placed in the water. He told Tagati that he would do whatever it took to get the power to take on the hyenas without the king. How he would save the kingdom and the people would make him king.

Tagati said, "I can help you defeat the hyenas. I can give you the power to wipe out entire villages. Is that what you would like?"

"Yes," Umholi said. "I want to wipe out whole villages of hyenas."

As he said this, there was a look of trance-like madness in his eyes. Tagati was taking over his will.

Tagati told him that he would have to pledge his soul to the Power of Darkness, and once he was in, he could not get out . . . alive.

Umholi wasn't interested in this so-called "pledge" as long as he would be a king. He agreed without contemplating the consequences. He basically sold his soul to the Devil.

Meanwhile, the small delegation sent out by the king came across the decomposing body of the messenger. All signs pointed to the poisoned water being the cause of his death. He looked to have been dead for almost a week. Immediately, they knew he had never made it to the hyena's land. This also meant that the hyenas did not know about the water problem.

The delegation sent one member back to the kingdom to notify the king that the messenger was found. The rest of the delegation kept moving forward to meet with the hyenas.

When the delegation member arrived back at the kingdom and was granted an audience with the king, he told him about the death of the first messenger and that the delegation continued on their way to meet with the hyenas. However, The King had news himself. The cause of the poison in the water was found to be some runoff from a nearby poisonous berry tree. The tree was dying, and when it rained, the berry juice found its way into the groundwater, from where the underground spring was sourced.

The king had already dispatched a crew to uproot and dispose of the tree. This would stop the flow of the berry juice and, with time, restore the water to a drinkable state."

Wepwawet: The Ruler of the Wolves

GG Pa continued, "Tagati told Umholi that he could help him take vengeance on the hyenas, but he could not make him king of the lions. He briefly explained that when he was expelled from the kingdom, it was by the gods. The expulsion came with a spell of protection for all the living creatures in the sunlight.

The spell the gods placed on Tagati also prevented him from leaving the planet's dark side. He would be destroyed if he left the dark side and crossed into the sunlight. And if he is destroyed, everything he created would also be destroyed.

Umholi was confused now. He said, "How can you help me if you cannot help yourself?"

Tagati told Umholi that he could make him "a king," but he would not be king of the lions.

Although this was not exactly the plan Umholi had dreamed up, he was willing to move forward with

Tagati's plan because he could still punish the hyenas. Additionally, he would be a king of sorts, just not in the lion kingdom.

He told Tagati, "Do what you must to make me a king of something. Then I will make myself the king of everything else."

Tagati motions for Umholi to sit on a large flat top stone just off the side of the semi-circle as he crushes some roots and berries. Once they are pulverized, he uses the mixture to paint Umholi's face. He is preparing him for the incantations to transform his body and spirit. Everything had to be done right to please The Lord of Darkness, Idemoni.

When the spell is complete, Umholi's soul will belong to Idemoni. Something Tagati forgot to mention to Umholi before they made the deal.

The Incantation begins with Tagati chanting and calling on the dark spirits to hear his call, over and over, until a strong wind swirls near them. A mist forms behind Umholi and gets denser by the second until it is more than the mist. It has thickened into a fog and thickens even more to be smoke-like. Tagati is now speaking in another tongue as he drops to his knees, and his eyes roll back into his head. The octaves of his voice go higher and higher each time he repeats the spell.

Umholi passes out, and the dark smoke envelopes him.

***

When the lion delegation arrived at the hyena cackle's settlement, they were met with hostile looks and attitudes. Since their distrust works both ways, the hyena security kept a sharp eye on them from the moment they arrived. Eventually, they were given an audience with the hyena's Vizier.

The delegation began with the usual greetings from the king, and then got straight to business. They told the Vizier about the groundwater issue back at the Lion Kingdom and how it had poisoned several of their people. They said to them that efforts were underway to determine the source of the poison, but the hyenas should be careful when drawing any groundwater from sources that flow from the East.

The Vizier thanked them for the information but asked why they had sent an entire delegation to deliver this news. Could the king not have sent a messenger? They let him know that a messenger had been dispatched two weeks earlier, but when he did not return, the delegation was formed to carry the news and to find out what had happened to the messenger.

The Vizier asked, "Did you find out what happened to the messenger?"

They replied, "Yes, it appears that he drank some of the tainted water along the way and perished before he had a chance to deliver his message."

The delegation packed up and thanked the hyenas for their hospitality. The hyenas thanked the lions for their visit and information. Then, the delegation headed home. Back to the kingdom. Relieved that the hyenas seemed to have no information on the poisoned water and were not aware of the issue, or so they said.

***

Umholi woke up, still feeling groggy but a lot different than when he first arrived. He knew that Tagati had painted his face, but somehow, it felt very different. He touched his face. His nose was sticking out further than before. And his ears were more prominent and pointier.

He used both of his hands to touch his head. It was then that he realized that he looked like a wolf. He had a wolf's head with a human body. How could that be? He was a Bevange, a lion hybrid. He can't be a wolf, too.

He tried to change into a lion but to no avail. He had lost his ability to morph. He was now a man with a wolf's head. His eyes were those of a demon, and he could feel that he was much stronger than he used to be. When he touched his mouth, there were the telltale fangs of the wolf.

He looked at Tagati, who smiled with satisfaction as he bestowed the name 'Wepwawet, god of wolves.'

There was still a lot of mist in the surrounding area, and it began to lighten up but not completely dissipate. As the fog thinned out wolves could be seen making their way slowly toward Wepwawet. First, there were two, then there were eight. Within two minutes, a pack of wolves, fifty deep, stood before him.

The wolves stood in lines as if they were soldiers in an army. They were some of the most enormous wolves ever. Their heads were four feet off the ground while they stood on all four legs. They were over seven feet long with huge paws. Their colors were not uniform, but they ranged from a dark grey to an almost true black. Their eyes were a demonic red to match that of Wepwawet.

His trepidation and anxiety vanished at the sight of the wolves. He now saw his condition as magnificent. The beginning of a new force to be reckoned with, and he was itching to get the fighting started.

Tagati opened a nearby chest and pulled out a collar of metal and forearm shields to be worn in battle. He gave them to Wepwawet. Then he picked up a dried stick from nearby. He held it out before himself and said a few unintelligible words. The stick straightened out and turned into a battle spear. Then he handed it to Wepwawet.

After handing him the spear, Tagati told Wepwawet, your new power is limited to the darkness. If the sunlight hits you, you will perish. That also applies to your army of wolves. So, any act of vengeance you would like to exact must be done in the dark, void of sunlight. You will need to wait for night to fall on the other side of the cave before trying to do anything and you must be back to the cave, in the dark, before the sun rises on you.

When darkness fell on the other side of the cave, Wepwawet and his army of wolves exited the cave, and he led them in the direction of the nearest hyena village he knew. It was the same one that the lion delegation had just left the day before.

The wolf army moved very fast and undetected through the wilderness. These wolves were extra-large and could move extra fast. Wepwawet himself could move at the speed of a wolf. They covered a lot of ground in a short amount of time. They were whizzing through grasslands and small forests with ease.

Within just two hours, they were just outside the hyena village, and they wasted no time. They pounced on the villagers, who were in complete shock. Most of them were already in their homes and their beds when the wolves burst in and began to tear them to shreds.

The wolves could not be stopped, and their speed made it impossible to be outrun. No man, woman, or child was to be spared. The long claws of the wolves made quick work of killing every inhabitant of the village. When all the killing was done, the wolves began to devour many of the fallen.

All the while, Wepwawet walked through the village proclaiming his coronation as King of the Wolves and how they would all pay. He stood tall and let out a loud and distinct howl while sticking out his chest. He could feel the power of his conquest over the village, building strength within his body. Then he kicked over the small campfires used for light and warmth, causing a small fire that began to spread. It spread enough to help some homes catch fire.

Wepwawet grabbed a young villager, who was trying to hide, by the throat, and while crushing his windpipe, he told him, "Tell everyone you encounter what happened here this night," before tossing him aside and allowing him to run off into the night.

It was all over in less time than it took to travel to the village. Several homes were on fire, and many bodies were strewn all over. Just that one hyena survived. Otherwise, the entire cackle was decimated. Wepwawet signaled for the pack of wolves to gather. Then he motioned, and they all began to run back to the cave.

In his mind, Wepwawet was very, very satisfied. He had exacted some vengeance on the Mafisi; to him, this was just a start. Once word about this got around to the others, not one hyena would ever feel safe, not even in their own homes."

The Delegation Returns

The villagers remained enthralled as GG Pa continued the story. "During the second night of the three-day journey, the lion delegation noticed a fire back in the direction from where they had just left the hyena settlement. They were about thirty-five miles away, and the fire still looked large, even from their distance. Going back to find out what was happening was not an option. They slept the night as best they could and continued home at first light.

By the end of the third day, the group was entering the kingdom grounds. Tired and hungry, they went to a dining hall before meeting with the king's council. They sat and ate a savory meal and had some delicious wine. The conversation turned to the smoke seen on the last night of travel. Everyone agreed this must be presented as very important to the council.

The delegation went to The Council Hall, where the council had already assembled. The leader of the delegation gave his report that the Mafisi Tribe was unaware of the groundwater being poisonous and was thankful that the delegation had come with a warning. The delegation felt that the Mafisi were sincere in their response.

The king thanked the delegation and informed them that the cause of the poisoned groundwater had been determined and rectified. He told them how the dead berry tree juices had seeped into the stream water and that the scientists could identify the source right after the delegation had left for the journey.

Before they could be dismissed, the delegation leader spoke up. He told the council that they had seen a large fire with heavy smoke coming from the direction of the Mafisi settlement just one night earlier. He emphasized how large the fire must have been for them to see it from almost 35 miles away. However, they did not sense any problems or issues in the Hyena village area.

The king looks around the council and realizes that his spiritual leader, Umholi, is absent. He asked, "Where is Umholi?"

No one answered. They looked at each other, puzzled.

The king asked, "Was he not summoned to the meeting?"

One council member responds, "I haven't seen Umholi for several days."

"Summon Mchawi," the king says. "And tell her to hurry."

It was twenty minutes before Mchawi arrived in the council chamber. The king instructed her to use her powers to see the past. Specifically, what happened in the Mafisi village on the previous night.

Mchawi begins her process of drawing a pentagram on the ground and placing a goat eye in the center. She starts her invocation and then falls into a trance. She waved her arms while swaying side to side, then back and forth. Suddenly, she stiffens up straight and tilts her head back, with her eyes open, without pupils or a cornea.

She says, "I can see the Mafisi village. It is nighttime, and shadows are moving extremely fast in the distance. They are moving fast toward the village. They enter the village and immediately begin destroying the village and the villagers. The hyena people are falling, . . . dead, all over. Some are being pulled from their beds, while others are being killed in their sleep. The attack is swift, vicious, and surgical. The Mafisi had no chance, and not one had a chance to morph before being killed."

"There is fire. And the fire is being used to burn the huts and halls. No one is left alive."

The king says, "Can you see what is killing the Mafisi?"

The witch says, "Wolves are being led by a Wolf King who calls himself Wepwawet."

"Wepwawet? Who the hell is that? Where did he come from?" said the king.

The witch says, "He is the one you call Umholi. He was transformed into a demon wolf god by Tagati."

"Tagati?" yelled the king. "And Umholi together?" "What the hell is going on?"

On Guard

GG Pa went on to describe how the deities, who were responsible for the planet's regeneration, were not pleased with Tagati for once again interfering with the natural progression of the inhabitants and for using Black Magic to eradicate the living. He had been confined to the planet's dark side, but now access between the forever dark side and the bi-light side (meaning that there is both sunlight and darkness) would need to be cut off completely.

Then, the deities appeared in the sky, and the clouds parted before a large dark cloud descended over the part of the planet that always remained dark. The ground shook violently and steadily for five or so minutes, and huge cracks in the earth began to form before a mountain began to rise out of the earth. This was unlike any other mountain because it went straight up in the air at a ninety-degree angle. It rose and rose until it reached the dark clouds and still rose some more, forming a colossal blockade between the two parts of the planet.

From what we knew, the mountain stretched around the circumference of the dark part of the planet.

The region was named M'Nayama, the home of demons and the evil they commit.

***

The villagers seemed stunned and sat quietly as if there was more to the story, but that was all GG Pa had to tell. The silence was deafening. The villagers were ignorant of this terrible part of their history.

Someone asked, "Why are we just learning of this?"

GG Pa said, "As far as I knew, this type of atrocity would never happen again after the boundary between the light and the dark was established. The horrible events, as described, sound very much like what happened so many years ago, but I cannot be sure they are related."

He continued, "The deities created the boundary to keep the 'Demons of the Dark' on the planet's dark side. It would take some powerful magic to break the boundaries. How they broke through and why now is of grave concern."

Bindi was at a loss for words or ideas. He stood there stunned at the story GG Pa had just told and was frightened by what it could mean for his family and the rest of the village.

He looked up to the sky as if he were ready to pray, but just off to the left of his position, he noticed a large bird in a giant tree. It was not just any large bird; he was sure it was the same bird the group had seen when they were in the Mafisi settlement. There it sat, looking down at the village and listening to the story of Wepwawet.

Bindi walked quickly over to Nuvu to corroborate the bird's identity. He tapped Nuvu on the shoulder and asked, "Is that the same bird from the Mafisi?"

When they both looked up to the tree, no bird was there. It was gone. Bindi said, "I swear, that bird was just up there."

Nuvu said, "If it was the same bird, why was it there and then flew away once you saw it?"

Balasu, another Elder, said, "If the wolves are still out there, and they are responsible for the devastation of the Mafisi settlement, our village will need to protect itself. Several village members must be on watch during the day and night. Maybe two shifts at night, so no one is overtaxed staying up so late. We must also set up tripwires to alert us of something moving in the dark. And the watchers must be armed with machetes and spears."

The villagers agreed and began making plans and volunteering for watch shifts. Everyone was scared, but there was no lack of courage. Protecting the village and the inhabitants was a badge of honor for them to lay down their lives for.

A Food Run

A few weeks had passed, and the time had come for the hunters to go back on a "food run." Although there had not been any new developments since the devastation of the Mafisi settlement, many villagers were still on edge. The hunting parties are always made up of many of the village's more agile and robust protectors. Sending them away for days was a concern for the people. The number of hunters in the party would need to be reduced, which meant not getting the village enough food to last as long. And, if the food ran out faster, the hunts would occur more often. This was a hard decision, but in the end, since there were no new attacks, the hunting party's numbers would not be diminished.

The hunters gathered as they usually would, according to the pre-arranged schedule. All their equipment and tools were in place and ready to go. It took a little longer for them to hug their families and say their goodbyes. Neither the hunters nor the villagers were sure they were making the appropriate decision. Not that they were leaving the village unprotected, because they were not. Just that they wanted to be there in case something happened.

The group finally fell in line and left the village on their way to hunt. The hunt leader encouraged them to clear their heads of negative thoughts to concentrate on making the kills out in the savannah. The group took off in a jog. They were running in cadence, almost like an old military unit.

The group was just a short distance from the hunting grounds by nightfall. They decided to camp around the large rocks obscured by overgrown grass and plant life. This strategic location would allow them to lie in the tall grass, hidden from prying eyes, and the rocks made a great perch for a lookout. Laying close to the rock, in the tall grass, made them look like they were just part of the landscape.

The savannah is a broad and vast area that is so large you cannot take in the entire view from any one spot. Many creatures, large and small, dwell in the savannah. And many animals, large and small, hunt in the savannah. Sometimes, the hunters can become hunted if they are not careful. Once the sun went down, it would generally be pitch dark out in the field, but this night would be different because it was just a couple of days away from the full moon, so there was a good amount of light in the night sky.

Many of the group had a tough time getting to sleep and knew how important it was to have plenty of rest before the hunt. Knowing you need sleep and shutting off your mind is not an easy task when worry is all around you—the worry of a family back at the village and their group out in the savannah.

Eventually, sleep finds each of them, and the campsite is quiet. Nothing is moving in the dark.

At first light, the hunters are already awake and ready for business. They stay put in the tall grass where they had slept the night before, waiting for an unsuspecting meal to show itself. And it did not take long before they saw a large herd of wildebeests running through the valley, just a thousand feet away.

The group breaks up instinctively. Everyone knew their part and did not need any instruction on what to do. The entire group morphed into their lion forms and split up to cut off the wildebeests' path and their potential escape route. There were so many of them that every hunter would catch at least one.

The lions crawled on their bellies to keep out of sight of the prey, and they moved slowly so as not to give away their presence. Some of the lions could already taste the flesh of the wildebeests in their mouths. Others were keenly tuned into the hunt and blocked out everything that could interfere with their concentration. The first row of wildebeests was now a hundred feet away.

When the herd had reached the thirty-foot mark, the lead row stopped abruptly, like a choreographed dance. Same steps, same head twist, and same attempt to escape. They sensed the presence of the lions, and almost immediately, they also saw the lions, who sprang out of the tall grass at a breakneck speed.

Every hunter was able to bring down a wildebeest, and a few caught two. Eleven wildebeest on day one made this a perfect hunting day. The group would spend much of the remaining hours of the day tying up the catch for transport and then resting up for the next day's hunt.

By sunset, the work of the first catch had been completed. The hunters were in good spirits, or at least not bad ones. They ate some of the catch and drank the good wine they had with them. They only sip the wine after the meal as a social bonding. When out in the field, there is no overindulgence. No one drinks to get drunk, just to bond with fellow hunters.

When the light of the almost full moon appeared, it quickly sobered them all anyway. They were all uneasy and wavering about staying away from the village, knowing that the past killings were somehow related to the full moon. The hunters agreed that they had caught enough food for the time being and would go home, at first light, with what they had. Additionally, there would be two lookouts per shift tonight.

Confronting Their Fears

It was the night before the full moon, and the villagers were enjoying some humorous entertainment after a hearty meal. Much of the humor was in their songs, which were very close to limericks with rhythm. The songs told stories of the village inhabitants and their challenges, small and large, much to the embarrassment of the subject.

It had been several weeks since the incident at the Mafisi settlement, and the tension in the village had subsided a lot, but not all the way. Keeping up with the familiar routines of the day and night helped everyone shake off the jitters. That's not to say that the sound of a twig snapping underfoot does not spark a sudden reaction, or at least a nervous twitch.

Just as the "party" was winding down, one of the spotters whistled as a warning. A quick hush came over the village like the way sounds suddenly stopped when you put your head underwater. Dancing, singing, and conversation halted in mid-cadence. Everyone froze in place as if standing still made them invisible. Or better yet, protected them from whatever would come. It's like playing dead, but you are still standing up.

It took just a few seconds to realize that the whistle was meant to draw their attention in the spotter's direction. As they all began to turn and look, someone yelled, "The strange light is back."

Yes, off in the distance, in what seemed to be the exact spot where they had seen the glow before, there it was again. It was almost as bright but just as eerie as it was before. A shiver passed through the people. The calm was gone. Fear had taken over again.

If this were to repeat the last occurrence, there would be a second light, a fire, in about an hour.

The countdown began. Ten minutes, twenty minutes, then thirty minutes. An hour, or at least what felt like an hour, finally came after what seemed like an eternity, but no second light. There was no fire in the distance that they could make out. However, the watch was not over because the first light, the eerie glow, was still there.

Although there was a shift schedule, no one was able to sleep. Anticipation had them on edge. When the glow began to dissipate; it did not ease their fear. When the glow stopped, they felt better.

The sun was rising, the moon was gone, and so was the eerie glow.

Nothing happened.

***

That evening, the hunters returned to the village. Their catch was light compared to their history, but the rest of the villagers quickly and quietly understood. Everyone was relieved to see the hunters return because this boosted the numbers to protect the village from the nameless beasts that were decimating communities. The fear was real, but it was not a long-range plan.

The villagers decided that they could not just sit around and wait to be slaughtered. Each night in the village was nerve-racking, as the unknown about what was out there terrified them. They had to find out what had happened to the Mafisi settlement and what that glow in the night had to do with it.

Fifty of the best fighters in the village were chosen. Both male and female. They planned to go out toward the area where the glow came from. They would only go some of the way but keep a distance far enough to survey the phenomenon without being seen by whatever, or whoever was causing it. Just observe and report back to the rest of the tribe.

The tribe gathered in The Great Hall, and all fifty of the fighters were blessed, individually and collectively, by the village Charmin. Each fighter was handed a sharp machete dipped in an ointment of slow healing. When the machete cut you, the wound would take months to heal if it ever did. This was meant to ensure that the enemy, who was cut with the blade, was mortally wounded and less likely to survive. Although they were going to observe, they had to be prepared in case of a fight.

After the rituals and eating a hearty meal, the group set out in the general direction of the glow. They believed it would be some time before the sun went down, which gave them enough time to travel and get into position before the glow began. They walked in formation, two by two, with Noola leading the way. Noola always wanted to be a soldier, and now he felt like he was one.

The group's direction did not have the most favorable terrain. After leaving the expanse of the village, they would enter sloping forest areas with steep ups and downs. The soil was somewhat loose, and the wrong step could send you sliding, so much caution was needed in the part of the forest. The trees were very large in both height and width; their lives must have begun with time itself.

Although it looked like one big forest, several forests were close to each other. Exiting the first tree line gave way to an open field about two thousand feet before the following tree line began. The open field was a welcome sight for the group since it was primarily flat and represented an achievement of making it through the precarious landscape of an ancient forest. It took much longer to get past the forest than they had prepared for, so they needed to catch up on their schedule, but they were also tired from the hike. They would rest here.

Six fighters were assigned the watch. Everyone else was able to sit and sip some water. Many ate from their rations of dried meats, but just a few bites since this was not a formal meal stop.

Back on their feet, they walked into the next forest. Right away, they sensed a presence. Noola passed the word through the ranks to be careful and watch for movement. Something about this forest didn't feel right.

The trees in this forest were not as large as the first forest, the canopies were lower, and the tree branches were closer to the ground. There were long vines loosely draped from tree to tree. The sun was still up, but the density of the trees prevented the sunlight from piercing the canopies. Nothing green was growing at ground level, but some strange-looking fruits were growing in the trees.

One of the fighters, Tata, pointed excitedly to something in a nearby tree. It was not a fruit; it was alive. As a matter of fact, it was a gorilla. Once the gorilla realized it had been discovered, it shrieked loudly to call other gorillas. And sure enough, gorillas began swinging and jumping through the trees from all directions. The fighters stopped in their tracks.

There now were gorillas everywhere, as far as the eye could see. The fighters were surrounded, but the gorillas stayed in the trees fifty feet away. Unmoving, they just peered at the group of fighters with curiosity while more and more gorillas filled up the trees on all sides.

Off to the left, the gorillas, small in stature, began separating. Making an opening in the "crowd" as five larger Silverback gorillas, swinging quickly through the trees, made their way to the group of fighters. They dropped from the trees one at a time and stood before the group.

It was evident that these gorillas were the leaders of the Troop. They were bigger and stronger looking than any of the other gorillas, and the one in the front acted as the absolute leader. The Silverbacks behind him were, most likely, his close relatives; they stood by his side but at least one step behind. Together, they probably made up the leadership of every gorilla family in that forest area.

At first, the Silverbacks' demeanors were light and non-threatening. They made a few light grunting sounds while looking Noola in the eye. The gorillas must have sensed, or assumed, that Noola was the leader since the group was following him and stopped on his motion, but there was no response from Noola to their "greeting."

The Silverback in the front grunted again, and still no response from the human group. It was not apparent to them that the group did not speak their language.

This time, the gorilla grunted much louder and beat on his chest. The other Silverbacks joined in, and the smaller gorillas in the trees began screaming and hooting. The gorillas started to advance toward the fighters.

The fighters didn't need an interpreter to understand this to be aggression, so when Noola raised his hand with the fight signal, all the fighters immediately morphed into their lion selves.

The speed at which the forest cleared was magical. The smaller gorillas disappeared as if they were never there, and the Silverbacks never looked back as they swung themselves furiously through the trees. The confrontation was over before it began. The gorillas didn't know that the humans they attempted to prey on were also lions and they were no match for the lions.

The fighters continued through this forest, sensing that the gorillas were still watching, but from exceptionally far away.

It took quite a while before the group of fighters emerged from the forest and into a clearing of tall, dried grass and weeds. This clearing was also rocky, with many large boulders scattered about, jutting out from the earth. All sizes stretched out over three or four hundred feet of open space.

The Battle for Their Lives

Noola quieted the group. "Sssshhhhh!!!, I hear something."

Everyone quickly quieted and listened intently. At first, there was nothing, but then they could hear a faint rumble. It sounded like a shallow swishing sound but slowly got louder. And not just getting louder but coming their way.

Tuta motioned for the group to get into position. They spread out and crouched down in the tall grasses, lying flat so as not to be seen by the approaching faction. No one knew what to expect because no one knew what was coming through the night. The villagers were lions at heart but humans by head, so there was a trace of fear of the unknown. The tension in the air was getting thicker and thicker as the sound got louder and louder.

Within a minute, the faint sound had become an unmistakable rumble, picking up volume. It was hard to distinguish any definitive features of the approaching group. Still, based on the clip of the gallop and the increasingly violent vibrations of the earth, there was no doubt that this was an army approaching.

The villagers sensed that the army was almost upon them. Machetes in hand and the set position, just one motion away from springing out of their hiding places. The time had come. The battle was at hand. They jumped out of the grass with the element of surprise, but it was the villagers who were surprised.

Coming at them extremely fast was an army of hybrid wolves, larger than any wolf they had ever seen. Although they had heard the story from GG Pa, these wolves were not the ones he described.

The army of wolves towered over the fighters from the village, and to make things worse, there were hundreds of wolves. These wolves ran exclusively on their hind legs and stood upright like men. Their bodies were covered entirely in fur, including their heads. Their hands were human, but they had claws. The kind of claws that could rip through flesh without resistance. They wore spiked armbands, body belts, and waist belts, just above a loin cloth. Each one had a battle spear as tall as they were and stood close to eight feet tall.

The fighters found themselves in a 'Do or Die' situation. There was no turning back now, so they attacked the approaching wolves. All except Nosoo, who decided to duck back down into the grass. He was terrified at the sight of the wolves and chose "flight" over "fight."

Unfortunately, the village fighters were no match for the wolves, who quickly grabbed villagers, still in their human form, by the head and pierced the torsos with their incredibly sharp claws. Then, they were lifted into the air and shaken enough to hear the bones of their spinal cord snap. Some died instantly, and others writhed in pain on the ground, paralyzed.

Other fighters could use their machete to affect a wound on their adversary, but it had no stopping power. Wolves were slapping the knives out of their hands with little resistance, then body slammed the fighters before adding a stomp. Others felt the sharp claws of the wolves slice through their bodies before not feeling anything anymore.

Those fighters, quick to morph into their lion forms, attacked the way they would attack prey in the fields, lunging at the wolves with claws out and swiping with their enormous paws. This created a snag for the wolves, who seemed unprepared to fight animals. The lions tore at the wolves, even drawing blood at times. They were quicker and more agile than they would have been in their human forms.

The lions fought well and inflicted actual harm on some of the wolves. Claws to the neck, body, and groin inflicted real pain, and the wolves who experienced this pain cried out with a howl of agony. That howl drew help from their friends, and together, they would take down the lion.

The fight was a mere distraction, and the wolves would not let it stop them from whatever plan they were about to carry out. Only a few of the wolves were tied up fighting with the lions, while the majority of them continued past the vicinity of the fight toward what must have been their original destination. The few village fighters also posed no threat to the wolves or their mission.

The entire fight lasted just a few minutes. The villagers were beaten to a pulp. Most of them were dead or dying.

***

Nosoo, lying motionless through the battle, slowly lifted his head after the commotion had died down for several minutes. He carefully looked around, only moving his eyes, trying not to draw any attention. To his delight, the wolves were gone, but his satisfaction ended there. All he saw next were the bodies of the dead fighters, who lay scattered about, still in lion form.

He looked around some more and realized there were just seven bodies out of forty-nine. He thought, "Where the hell did the rest of them go?"

Just then, he felt the ground shake and heard the same rumble when the wolves first showed up. He morphed into his lion form and ran off as fast as he could back toward the village. Not considering any known or unknown dangers, he was getting out of the way of those wolf-like creatures. He had to get back home and warn his people.

Along the way, he did reencounter the family of Silverback gorillas, but he was running so fast they didn't even bother to confront him. The biggest gorilla just looked in his direction as Nosoo came and went before he could even stand up.

Nosoo ran for miles before he finally slowed down to take a breather. He knew the journey back to the village would take more than a day, but he was determined to cover as much ground as possible.

When Nosoo arrived at the village, he was in a panic. A panic so bad that he frightened the villagers with his demeanor alone. He was out of breath from running so fast and so far, but he was also trying to speak while breathing hard. His stuttering and the stress of his speech made it impossible to understand him. The people of the village coaxed him to stop talking, take a breath, and drink some water before trying to talk.

Mourning the Dead

There was no need to use the horn to call the people together because word about Nosoo's return spread fast. The villagers were coming from all directions, walking fast or outright running.

After he had calmed down just a bit, he told them the events of the journey. Specifically, the battle with the wolf-like creatures was less of a battle and more of a slaughter. He described the terrifying beasts and how they made short work of the Imbube fighters. He also told them the creatures already had a destination because they didn't allow the fighters to deter them from their objective.

The villagers stood in awe. They were shocked by the story they just heard. You could have heard a pin drop in the dirt, no less. Then, the crying began, and the tears started to flow. Some screamed out their lost loved one's name. It was pandemonium for about five whole minutes. The news was too much for many of them. Fifty fighters went out, and just one returned.

After the initial chaos subsided, Nosoo was asked how he could make it out alive. He told them that he panicked and hid when he saw the creatures. The people were angry with him, and a few called for him to be severely punished for being such a coward, but cooler heads prevailed. They realized that if he didn't get away, the village would never have known about the creatures, and they would either send more people to their deaths looking for the first group of fighters, or they would never have known what happened to their loved ones.

***

The battle was over, but the war had just begun. The wolf-beasts had retreated, yet they had no explanation for why or where. The wolves were clearly in control of the momentum. Their strength seemed almost impossible, and their teeth cut through flesh as easy as eating a banana. Not to mention that the lions were severely outnumbered and sorely mistaken about their ranks, but why did the wolves retreat when they did, and where did they go before they retreated?

These questions will have to wait as they collect the bodies and pieces of the dead fighters.

The long trek back to the battleground was much longer than when the fighters first went because the recovery team needed to bring wheeled carts to retrieve the dead, so they had to take the longer, safer route. Also, Nosoo didn't want to run into those gorillas again. He had described the encounter to the others, and they agreed to avoid the forest that housed the gorillas.

When the recovery group arrived back at the field, bodies and body parts were scattered all about the once pristine oasis. Large swaths of the landscape were covered in blood and mud. You could see where the wolves had dragged away many fighters. There was a clear path of flattened grasses, broken shrubbery leading off to the East, and the "all telling" trails of blood.

This was a most humiliating defeat. They were taken down by an enemy they didn't even know they had.

The walk back to the village, with the few bodies they could recover, seemed much longer than any of the other walks to or from the field. Nosoo would describe himself as he trudged back home to the village as wounded, broken, and disillusioned.

After arriving home again, they took the recovered bodies to the Great Hall, where they would be prepared for burial.

Funerals at the village were not elaborate, and they did not use caskets. The body, or bodies, are merely placed into a hole in the ground at the tribal burial site. This is the first time that we have had more than one person to bury, and just as important, the bodies were in the lion form. When people have died in the past, they were in human form, and they died of a natural cause, but this would be different. If you are killed, you remain in the form in which you were killed.

Each body was laid out on a blanket provided by the family. They agreed they would be positioned on their stomachs and posed as if asleep in the grass. Paws beneath them, head pointed straight, chin down, and their tails curled beneath them.

Each body was rubbed with scented oil to keep the decaying smell from penetrating the burial plot. Then, their fur and manes were brushed as if they were getting ready for a night out.

Then, one at a time, they were lifted onto a cart. Each one had their own cart. Then, the procession to the burial grounds began. It was a sorrowful sight; the people of the village were broken, and many were inconsolable. They had lost many people who made the village what it was. They were providers and protectors of their families, and now they were gone. Jvonn was inconsolable when he saw the body of his father, Konni, being laid to rest. His mother and GG Pa were as saddened by his loss as they were by their own.

The burials didn't take long, and the people were back at the village in time for dinner, which could just as quickly have been considered a repast. The meal was very somber, and many were still crying or sniffling. The pain from this considerable loss would take a long time to ease, and it would never heal. The loss was huge to such a small community.

Forever Changed

That evening, after dinner was over and most had returned to their homes, Nosoo spoke with some of the villagers he knew would still be at the Great Hall.

Nosoo was having trouble letting go of what had transpired. He also felt very guilty for being the only one to survive the slaughter, and that was due to his cowardice. Their pride was their bond, and losing his pride was devastating.

Walking over to the Great Hall, he stared blankly at the sun settling off in the distance. This evening, it looked more like a ball of fire or a hot, fiery, blood-filled eye staring at him accusingly.

The village was quiet and still. Where young ones would typically be playing and running, there was just quiet. There was just empty quietness where many would generally be moving and milling about. The village was forever changed.

When Nosoo arrived at the hall, much of his anger turned into despair, and the burning fire in his eyes had been reduced to a smoldering, like an old rope, as it burned out.

Just four villagers were in the hall when Nosoo arrived, and they were deeply engaged in conversation. The discussion was loud and animated. Opinions were strong, but only one could prevail. There has been clearly one winner so far, GG Pa, Jvonn's great-grandfather.

Tomas was pleading his case to remain in the village. "GG," he said, "we walked for days on end before we came upon this land, and I don't want just to turn and leave so easily."

Maneek quickly pointed out, "We know what transpired those many years ago, when Umholi made his pact with Tagati, and how the Mafisi were slaughtered." he said. "Now we are facing a similar threat. Do we want just to sit here and wait for it to come to us?"

GG Pa added, "Also, considering how easily many of our best fighters were killed and the description of the Wolf Army, I see no choice for us other than to get as far away from this area as we can."

Tomas added, "Those were the exact words you used when we first left the Imbube Kingdom. Now you are using them to rationalize a return."

When Nosoo's presence was noticed, the discussion stopped suddenly, allowing him to get closer and join in. He was greeted customarily and offered a refreshment.

Once the pleasantries were done, Nosoo was brought up to speed on the fiery conversation. There were three options to be considered, and one was suicide.

GG Pa asked, "What other options do you see for our people?"

The first idea was to gather all the adult members of the village, numbering about one hundred ten, and go back out to the battle site and wait for the wolves to return. The villagers would fight to the death to avenge their fallen tribe members. This would also require the village Elders to gather all the youngsters, lead them out of the village, and head to the Kingdom of Imbube.

The second idea was for everyone to continue sitting tight in the village and keeping up the security watches that had been in effect for almost two months. This idea would allow the village to continue, but not as usual. The anxiety of the unknown, which had taken hold in the village since the massacre at the Mafisi settlement, was unnerving, to say the least. Continuing to live in the village would no longer be the same.

They could call it home, but the home-like feeling would not be there.

The third idea was to pack up and leave. Knowing that the village and the villagers were no longer safe, it made sense to abandon their home of forty-plus years. Staying put would feel like they were just waiting for death. Some young people had not yet begun to live their lives, and some were just beginning to live theirs. There has already been a life-changing event that has inflicted a permanent wound on this society, so it makes sense to put distance between the people and the heartbreak while taking the people to a safer location.

When the debate was finished, GG Pa declared, "It is settled. Everyone will leave their homes and travel to the Kingdom of Imbube."

The group was going through the five stages of grief, but some were moving through them faster than others. The ones stuck in denial wanted to stay put, while the ones who had moved on to anger wanted to take revenge, but overall, bargaining for continued life was winning the day. The preservation of the tribe was more important than vengeance or ignorance. The decision was made to uproot the people and form a caravan to trek hundreds of miles to the Kingdom. An announcement would be made in the morning, and the actual move would occur in a week.

This was not the outcome that Nosoo wanted, but he, too, realized that this was not about him alone and that the continued existence of the tribe was of the utmost importance. He agrees with the decree on the outside but seethed with vengeance on the inside. And when the group broke up to return to their homes, he kept thinking, "How could things have gone so wrong?" "Who, or what were those things that killed all of his friends?" "Where did they come from?"

These nagging questions and the fact that he ran from the fight made it much more disturbing. Knowing that the rest of the village, who had lost their fathers, mothers, and children, knew that he hid during the battle made it awkward as well. There was no way he could continue to live among the villagers and hold his head up high. He had to leave the village.

**

The following day, during a special breakfast meeting, the four Elders who had met in the hall the previous night took center stage. GG Pa informed the villagers that their comfortable lives in "paradise" had ended. The new developments with the slaughter at the Mafisi settlement, as well as the slaughter of their own fighters, created a severe threat to the Imbube people.

Therefore, remaining in the village is no longer safe, and we must seek help and shelter. Everyone is to pack up their homes and prepare to relocate to the Kingdom of Imbube.

The murmurs began quickly, and many were not pleased by the announcement, but they also knew that the elders were right. The village was susceptible to being overrun and destroyed by the army of evil on the loose, but the idea of going to the kingdom was just as scary. Many were young when they left and did not remember the kingdom. Most of the others had never been to the kingdom, and the anxiety about going there was real.

Once everyone calmed down and the grievances subsided, the instructions were given to be ready in two days. The villagers were instructed not to bring more than they could safely carry nor to bring extras or personal belongings that were not absolutely necessary. The walk will be long, and the terrain will be rugged in some places. The entire walk could take approximately 24 days, at a steady clip, the approximate number of days before the full moon reappears. They did not want to escape the village, only to be executed in the open fields.

They were all dismissed so that they could go to their homes and begin packing up. Unfortunately,

Nosoo did not feel it the way the others did. His mind was still not right, and it continued to race all the while he walked to his home. And when he reached his home, he didn't go inside. He didn't even stop walking. He just walked on by and kept going.

***

When the sun rose on the second day, the day of departure, Nosoo was still not accounted for. His family was deeply concerned since he had been missing for two days, but his wife knew of his despair and the weight of his collapse on the battlefield. She hoped that he would return to the village before the procession left, but no such luck. She hid her fear from the children, but deep down, she was scared about what her husband might do or be trying to prove. She also knew that she could not waver in her responsibilities to her family, and that meant keeping the children safe. The three took their packs and joined the others at the Great Hall.

After a hearty breakfast and a few words of guidance, the group gathered outside the hall, picked up their belongings, and started the long, twenty-plus-days journey to the Kingdom of Imbube.

A Long Walk

The caravan of villagers had just completed their first day of the long journey to The Kingdom of Imbube. The pace of the march was reasonable for a group of hybrid lions, where a full-blooded human might have had trouble. However, the journey had just begun, and no one knew what to expect. From the current perspective, the road ahead is endless.

Although they were called The Elders, GG Pa and his three cohorts, Maneek, Shuja, and Tomas, moved with agility and purpose. They knew when to turn, and they knew when to stop. They knew how to keep the group together and in coordination. Every time the group would leave from a pit stop, certain people were placed at specific points on the line of travelers, which proved to be ideal and strategic to keep the group moving while keeping the group aware of any potential threats.

The Elder's leadership and logistics on this undertaking were almost flawless. Except for the fact that none of the group had been this far away from their village in more than thirty years, everything seemed to be unchanged in all the years gone by. However, everyone knows that nature makes its changes and does not ask permission. What "once was" is not guaranteed to "still be."

The leaders signaled that the group would rest here for the night and get a fresh start on the hill in front of them in the morning. Everyone gathered to eat. In their prearranged circles, similar to the Great Hall at home. Dinner on the road would not be as elaborate as in the village, but only the youngsters would gripe. The adults knew how different things would be while traveling, so they accepted the lack of specific amenities without so much as a moan. The really young ones had no idea that anything was different, and they really didn't care.

The group would remain just outside of the tree line to their left. Not too close as to be caught off guard by any intruders. Sentries were placed around the campsite, and a limited calm came over the people as they went to sleep. The sentries were relieved by others in the group every couple of hours so everyone could get a decent amount of sleep.

The night passed without fanfare, much to the relief of all.

After a good breakfast, the caravan was reconvened, and the group set off again.

***

It was close to sundown on the fourth day of travel when they reached the crest of a miles-long hill. It was not a very steep hill but a very long one. When Jvonn looked back from the top of the mountain, he could see for miles and also realized that the group was now above the tree lines of the forest behind them, where they had stopped to rest before. He was excited since he had never been this high up to see over the trees. He would have loved to run amok and laugh, as any young child in the group, but they were all corralled in the middle of the caravan to keep them protected and moving in the right direction.

The group broke into their campsite mode and prepared for their evening meal. GG Pa and his pals gathered on the side to have a discussion. Although several group members saw the elders' gathering, no one tried to intrude because they knew whatever they were discussing was essential to the trek.

The Elders discussed the plan for the coming days and how the group would maneuver through the coming challenges, including the following feat. What goes up must come down.

After climbing such a long and rising hill, they would need to descend, but the down was less friendly than the up. The down was much more abrupt and demanding. It would be a steep descent over some loose and rocky ground. With many group members not yet experienced in climbing and descending this type of terrain, a plan would be necessary, especially since there was a river at the bottom. If anyone lost their footing, to the extent that they rolled down the hill, they would definitely end up in the fast-moving river.

The Elders decided it would be prudent to walk the edge of the slope, just before the down slope, to see where the least dangerous spots would be and to map out the trail they would use. During this scouting, they saw an area that could serve as a natural trail. If walking diagonally, this portion of the hill could be the best way down, and it stretched the entire length of the hill. The whole two miles down the path was more than wide enough to accommodate the group walking in single file. The rains probably carved it out, but now it will serve as a footpath for these travelers.

When the three returned to the rest of the group, they were just in time for the evening meal and were very happy about that. Each of them grabbed some food and then continued to sit together and discuss the continuing plan. Although the path was wide enough, it was still slightly steep, and the travelers carried their belongings and supplies. It was agreed that this still presented a challenge to the task, but they were well-equipped to mitigate the risks.

The Elders called a meeting once the meal was finished, and everyone finished their after-dinner cleanup. Maneek, instead of GG Pa, led this meeting. Although GG Pa was usually the spokesperson of The Elders, he sat back and allowed one of his cohorts to take center stage this time, sending a message of cohesion to the rest of the traveling villagers. The message was when these men talk, it is in unison, and their words should be adhered to.

Maneek began by thanking everyone for their attention and saying how important the next week would be to their trek to the Kingdom of Imbube.

Maneek said, "Tomorrow, we will begin the descent from this elevation in the mountain to a lower elevation that is not a valley, but just a level that is lower than this one. That means there will come a point where we will again need to descend, still lower, to get to the bottom of the mountain and into the valley. I want you all to understand that nothing about reaching the valley will be easy or safe. We must be careful and mindful every step of the way."

Maneek continued, "Tomorrow, at first light, we will eat an early meal and begin the walk down the hill. The path is reasonably wide, but the ground is not entirely firm. This means we will encounter areas where the soil can move and challenge our footing. Should one of us slip the wrong way, they could roll down the hill and into the fast-moving river below. We do not want that. We also do not want anyone to slip and cause others to fall with them. Therefore, everyone must change into their lion or half-lion form to have the best chance of successfully making it down the path."

He instructed them to wrap their belongings and supplies in a fashion that would allow their lion form to transport the parcels easily. They would need to attach and tie them to their bodies. The best way to approach this would be to have several people stay human while they help their neighbors and family get their packages in place and then help each other until the last person has morphed.

He asked whether there were any questions, and there were none.

He then called for the first shift of night sentries to take their positions and wished everyone a good night before the group dispersed.

Most of the group began bedding down for the night, but some were still not tired. Whether it was nerves or anxiety, it was just not time for them to go to bed yet, so they gathered together to talk amongst themselves.

***

When the sun began rising over their encampment, one-third of the people were already preparing. They were doing their best to keep themselves moving and engaged, not to lose their spirit. Leaving their home, the only home they have known for all, or most, of their lives, was not simple. It was the most challenging thing they had ever done.

In keeping with the previous night's instructions, after breakfast had been eaten and everything had been packed away, the group began loading their belongings on their backs, like the packs on a mule or horse. The first people to be loaded up were those who could fully morph into lions since they would walk on all fours. Then, the remaining group of half-hybrids helped each other load their packs on their backs.

Once they were ready, the group leaders motioned for them to begin the trek down the hillside path. The lineup was much the same as the preparations; entirely morphed lions, even the children, would go first. Each individual was spaced out by ten feet and told to maintain their distance from the person in front of them. This was imperative to prevent a cascade of bodies in case someone fell or slipped down the steep terrain.

The trail down the mountain slope began just a few feet away from a large boulder that looked like a piece of the mountain jutting up from the edge of the peak. This was a good landmark that could also be seen from the bottom.

When the first group began their descent, they quickly noticed that the Elders were positioned at several points along the down route, and GG Pa was already at the bottom. He helped coordinate the troupe as they descended, and the other Elders assisted each traveler in moving through areas that may otherwise prove tricky or deadly.

The descent went very well, and everyone was off the top landing. Small rumbles were felt in the side of the hill, with many of the group already down the embankment and the last of them just over a hundred feet up. Dirt and small rocks were sliding down from the top, gaining speed all the way down. This was not good.

The people at the bottom started moving away from the area where the dirt and rocks were most likely to land, but the part of the group still on the trail was in the path of the slide. Everyone was thinking, just like any other mountain slide, it all begins small and grows into a landslide. This predicament had all the hallmarks of something that could develop into a disaster, and the people still on the path needed to get down to the landing post haste.

The Elders beckoned to the group on the landing to keep moving away from the area where the dry dirt and small rocks were beginning to show signs of piling up while urging the balance of the crowd, still making their way down, to hurry. It was time to throw caution to the wind and do everything possible to hurriedly get everyone off the trail before the situation became dire.

Maneek, standing off to the left of the trail at the bottom, looked up to the top of the slope to see if there was any indication of what might be causing this sediment cascade. Then, he saw a group of elk near the edge, at the top of the slope, on the landing, but they were looking over. There was nothing special about that, but just a few yards over to the right, he could see what looked like a huge antler, and it was hammering at the giant boulder the group used as a landmark.

Maneek called over Tomas and pointed to the enormous antler. Tomas quickly ran over to GG Pa and Shuja to warn them.

The rest of the villagers were reaching the bottom of the trail, and everyone hurriedly got away from the area just in time before some much larger pieces of the hill began to roll down and create a pile-up on the landing. There was a significant buildup of dirt and rock almost ten feet high. The pile needed to be more significant to stretch out as far as the width of the entire landing so none of the dirt made it into the river.

The group gathered a short distance from the landslide, out of harm's way, to assess any damages. Everyone changed back to their human forms. For the most part, everyone was reasonably unharmed, except for a few minor bruises from having to jump, tuck, and roll before they were ready. However, no one was killed, and that could have been a distinct possibility had they not jumped into action when they did.

While the whole caravan gathered to dust themselves off and speculate on the cause of the landslide, the Elders were off to the side, discussing the usually large antler they observed at the top of the mountain as the landslide was happening. They concluded that this was not a natural occurrence and that something may have been trying to kill them. They would have to be on heightened alert from this moment on.

Nosoo Finds Clues

It had been at least two weeks since Nosoo had left the village without telling anyone. He had made up his mind that he could not continue to live with his people while feeling the kind of shame he was feeling. He thought others, undoubtedly, looked down on him as a coward for hiding during the battle with the wolf army, and even if they didn't consider him a coward, he considered himself a coward.

He had finally made his way back to the place where the slaughter occurred. He calls it a slaughter now because there was no battle, let alone a fight. The giant half-wolf creatures had decimated the lion fighters with barely any effort, and most of their wolf army kept moving by without stopping to engage them. They knew that the fighters were of no consequence to their mission, so it took little effort to quickly dispatch the meddlers.

Nosoo looked around and surveyed the area. He stood utterly immobile as he stared straight ahead. In his mind's eye, he could still see the wolf army tearing apart his friends and relatives. He almost felt like he was reliving the horrors of that night, even in the daylight. It still felt so real that he panicked again and dived for cover. He lay there with his head down, unmoving, as if trying to be invisible. It wasn't long before he realized his lunacy because there was nothing, and no one, here to be afraid of. It was all just a memory. It is a vivid memory, but a memory, nonetheless.

Time and weather had cleared many of the signs of the massacre, like the blood pools and stains, but yet there were still some faint signs. Nosoo stood by an area where the blood pool was so large that even the remnants of it were very evident. He broke down and cried. He didn't know exactly whose blood it was, but he did know it was symbolic of everyone who died that day on this battlefield.

After he had finished with his crying, his anger kicked up. He looked around, looking for something in particular, but he didn't know where it was. He looked hard to the right and then hard to the left before looking to his right again. He stood up and took a few paces to the right, where he reached down to touch a broken branch. Then, as if a light bulb came on, he saw swatches of broken branches leading back into the direction the wolves had taken during their retreat after they returned from wherever they had gone in the first place. The wolves had left a trail he could follow, and Nosoo would use that trail.

***

The trail Nosoo was following had taken him in several different directions over the last few days, and many turned out to be dead ends, but he would backtrack each time to where the trail branched off and take another branch. He was determined to find the wolves' lair and do something about it. He had no idea what exactly he would do, but it would be something.

The trail had taken him through some dangerous parts of the forest, where he had to creep stealthily through so as not to be discovered by the locals. He was lucky enough to avoid those pesky gorillas at one point. He was fortunate not to have been detected by the tribe of wild boars who passed within yards of his hiding place. Although he could morph into a lion, he was only one lion, and the numbers were against him.

The trail had taken him to the edge of a lake before some of it disappeared, but a part of the trail went along the banks of the lake. He followed the tracks around the lake's edges, which made more sense since he needed to know where they entered or exited the lake. The lake was also a major source of drinkable water, and he could use a drink.

He began to recognize that he was getting closer and closer to the dark clouds and the colossal mountain, and every time he looked in that direction, every hair on his body stood up, and chills ran down his spine, but he kept going anyway. The anger and determination drove him, and he would not allow his fears to overtake control.

He only had to walk around part of the lake's circumference before finding where the trail picked up again. The trail on this side of the water was much more pronounced and direct. The origin point was definitely the mountain. He would have to be on the lookout for any signs of movement while also being very careful not to be caught snooping because that could be the end of him if he is caught.

Nosoo changed into his lion form and guardedly crept closer and closer to the mountain, all the while following the trail of sparse blood drops and plant life that had been trampled underfoot. In this area, there was a lot of trampled plant life, which indicated that a large number of beings had moved through the area, but there was no telling how long ago since their movement.

When Nosoo reached the foot of the mountain, it was more like the foot of a cliff. A cliff that rose straight up into the air on an angle close to 90 degrees, and there were no hand or foot holes to permit climbing. Looking up, the cliff rose high into the sky, thousands of feet, until it disappeared into the dark black clouds. The top of the cliff, or mountain, was not visible, so there was no telling how high the mountain was or if this really was a mountain at all. The cliff face stretched to the left as far as the eye could see and kept going. This was the same for the right side. And what bothered Nosoo more than anything else was that there was no opening to the cliff at the bottom.

The trail ended right here at the face of this cliff, but where could they have gone from here? Even the paw prints ended here, indicating that the beasts who made them went through the mountain wall. "How was that possible?" he asked himself as he touched the absolutely solid rock face of the mountain. "There must be more to this, and I will not rest until I find out," he thought.

Nosoo sat down to think and ponder his situation. He was alone in a strange land of unknown origin, on the doorstep of an unknown force with evil intentions toward him and his kind. Why? That, too, is unknown.

He realized that there were a lot of unknowns to his circumstances, and it may be best if he did not sit smack dab in front of the mountain, just in case the wolves returned or reappeared from wherever. He saw a tree line a few hundred feet away, and the trees were huge. This would be a suitable place to lie low and keep out of sight.

***

Nosoo figured he would build a small encampment up against one of the giant trees, but not one on the very edge., so he wouldn't be too close and easily identified by whatever came from the mountain. He gathered together branches and large leaves, along with some moist soil. After digging a hole about four feet wide, four feet long, and just two feet deep, he used some leaves to line the bottom. He used the twigs and branches to create a makeshift wall along a portion of the perimeter, and some of them were used, along with the large leaves, to fashion a partial roof to the space. Once he was finished, he had a space where he could crawl in and sleep, away from prying eyes, if there were any, and he could be undetected by whatever might come browsing through the area.

By now, Nosoo was exhausted. It had been a long day with all the work. He had yet to eat a full meal during his travels, so he would need to go out and find food before calling it a day. He thought about the lake. He did see some fish when he was there earlier, and he needed to fill his canteen again anyway. So off he went to get some water and catch a fish for dinner.

He returned to the lake, canteen in one hand and short spear in the other. He didn't bring a lot of tools with him when he ran away from the village, but he would use the tools he had to the best of his ability. The kind of fishing he was used to requires a string and a hook. A wooden hook, but a hook, nonetheless. Spearfishing would be a new skill to master, and if he wanted to eat, he needed to learn fast.

When he entered the water, he was amazed at how cold it was. This was supposed to be a sliver of paradise, and the water temperatures are usually a bit warmer. He was immediately curious as to where the source of this lake was. He glanced around on all sides, but there was nothing immediately visible. He surmised that the source could be from below the surface.

He walked out into the water until it reached just above his knees. This, he thought, would be deep enough to catch a fish. He raised his short spear, so his fist was just above his shoulder blade, and he stood perfectly still as he waited for an unsuspecting fish to wander into his kill zone.

Several times, a fish had come into the kill zone, and Nosoo plunged his spear into the water but failed to catch the fish. This method of fishing was a bit harder than he anticipated, but he was not going to give up because he already had the taste for fish in his mouth. "If at first you don't succeed, try, try again," he could hear in his head, and he was going to keep trying.

As he stood there, still, unmoving, and just slightly cold, a reasonably sized fish was swimming just outside the kill zone. Nosoo gathered all his wits about him as he stiffened every muscle in his body. He told himself, "Not yet, not yet," as he waited for the fish to get closer and into the kill zone. The fish must have been telling himself, "Not there, not there," because he kept skirting the zone before swiftly pulling back and swimming out of reach.

This fish seemed to be playing with Nosoo by swimming up close to the kill zone and then swimming back away, and he was the only fish coming near. It was almost as if the entire fish community was in on the joke, and they had sent this fish in on a dare that he was more than happy to take on. The game was called 'Tease the Fisherman,' and the goal was to keep taunting the stalker and drive him mad.

The game was going well for the fish, and Nosoo was getting increasingly frustrated. He was losing his mind, trying to stand completely still and unmoving. The fish, once again, was swimming close to the zone, just outside the invisible line, when abruptly, and in a flash, Nosoo morphed into a lion and swiped the naive water dweller, catching him in the claws of his paw, as he mutters the words, "mother chucker."

Nosoo had his meal for the evening, and he felt triumphant as he made his way out of the lake. When he turned to look back at the water, he thought he saw something in the middle of the water, so he stopped to look.

Nothing moved. No ripples to indicate movement. No sign of anyone or anything. Nosoo turned and kept walking back to his campsite.

Once his back was turned and he was moving away, the water did ripple, and something substantial moved away, under the water, in a different direction. It had been watching Nosoo in the water fishing the entire time. It had been standing still, waiting, stalking, but now it just moved on and swam away.

Onward

The next leg of the journey would require the group to cross a river. Since this was not an area they frequented nor were familiar with, they had no name for the river, but they could plainly see that trying to cross it would be a challenge. The immediate location where they were standing would not work because the water was moving too fast, and they could eyeball the fact that it was a very deep point. The group must walk downstream and identify a safe location to cross.

Kima, one of the women in the group, turned to her friend Ey'lona and asked, "What is your take on all of this? We have no idea where we are going or what to expect when we get there."

"All I know is that we lost our husbands, and it is our motherly duty to save our children," Ey'lona said.

Kima nodded in agreement but still felt that her question was not answered.

The day was still young, so there would still be a lot of travel time, so the group leaders aroused the travelers to their feet. The excitement of the landslide was over, and it was time to keep moving. They were told to grab their gear and fall in line as the leaders began moving out, walking along the river, and observing the current for a safe location to cross. At the same time, they were also looking up to the top of the mountain above their heads, keeping an eye out for any more landslides or what may have caused the landslide.

The group had been walking downstream almost an hour before they saw an area where the river widened significantly, and the flow was slowed. There were also some visible fish, just the right size for eating. The Elders brought the group to a halt and announced that they would cross here.

The area closest to the banks was shallow, so everyone could walk out to the area where the water began to get deeper. The tallest of the group were asked to go out and see how deep the water might get. When one of the tallest villagers made it out to the middle of the river without the water reaching his chin, they realized that this was probably the best they would ever come across, and it was ideal to cross here.

The river's current, in the middle, was still a little strong, so they decided to form a human chain with the taller villagers in the middle. Everyone in the chain would be in size place, and they would stretch the chain from the point in the river where the water rose to three feet and would extend to the other side of the riverbank where the water was also three feet. The members of the chain locked arms to make the chain strong.

The travelers would use the human chain to hold onto as they crossed to help them keep their heads above the water and to help keep them from getting caught in the current and dragged away, and it was working perfectly. That is until someone lost their grip on one of the children. The child floated away and floated fast. Then, the adult was also swept away by the current.

"Quickly," said Maneek, pointing to two adults on the riverbank, "follow them and help get them out of the water."

The group panicked immediately, and the coordination began to break down. The Elders quickly told the chain to stay in place so the crossing could continue while two adults ran down the riverbank behind the floaters.

The water was moving very fast. Faster than the rescuers could run, they kept the two floaters in sight as much as possible, but there was a turn, and they lost sight. The run was long, but there was a stroke of luck.

The river widened again, and the water slowed and spread out. The youngster had changed into its lion form and could stand on all four feet and walk out of the river onto the riverbank. The adult floater was able to grab hold of a large rock and stop her movement before standing up in the water, which was just over three feet at that spot.

The two of them were already walking on the riverbank, back upstream, when the rescuers came running. They gave them the once over and asked if they were hurt. Then, they all began the walk back to the rest of the group.

Once they were all back together and all on the appropriate side of the river, they identified a good spot to rest and have lunch before resuming the journey.

***

Everyone was so relieved that the young child had survived the river ordeal, and everyone also had their own opinion as to who was at fault, but none of that was important now. The next leg of the journey would be through a forest. A forest that no one remembers being in. It must have grown during the last forty or fifty years, so this must now be treated as unfamiliar territory and every precaution must be taken.

The Elders had a good idea of which direction the group needed to go, but that was it, just a good idea. They would instinctually make it through the trees and come out on the other side. The travelers regrouped and headed out. The group had some sluggishness since they had begun early in the day and already had two challenging obstacles to overcome, the mountain downslope and the river. The mysterious forest was an "unknown," but the hope was that it posed no danger to the people.

Moving through the forest was relatively easy. It may have been because the relatively new tree line had yet to accumulate all the naturally occurring insects and animals that would typically inhabit a forest. Or, more likely, since this entire new world was less than 300 years old, the forest animals did not yet exist. Or should I say, exist anymore? Or maybe they spoke too soon.

Off to the group's left, a few hundred yards away, stood a group of twenty or more full-grown elk. They were big and healthy. From a distance, they looked like some of the larger elk with thick fur around their thick necks that almost looked like they were wearing a turtleneck sweater. Tomas estimated their height to be close to six feet. These were some truly large elk, but why were they just standing there looking at the villagers?

The Elders told the group to keep moving and avoid antagonizing the elk. So, the group moved on.

A few minutes later, one of the organizers from behind the group hurried forward to inform the Elders that the elk were following the villagers.

When the Elders stopped to look, as the group kept moving, they could see the elk off in the distance, following their path. This was a strange behavior for elk. Typically, elk want to be left alone to graze and frolic, but not this bunch, they were paying no attention to the greenery. Their eyes were on the villagers.

Several villagers laughed at the elk, saying, "If only they knew they could end up as dinner for us."

That may be true, GG Pa thought. Maybe they have never come across humans way out here in this area. Especially since the villagers were probably the only humans this far out from the kingdom, the elk may have no idea they were prey. It would soon be time for dinner, and some fresh meat could go a long way toward shaking off the stresses of this challenging journey.

Shujaa whispered to Maneek, "Those elk look like a well-deserved dinner for the people."

Shujaa agreed and brought their concerns to the other Elders.

It was decided that the travelers would take advantage of this situation and use it to benefit themselves. Ten villagers were chosen, or volunteered, to form the hunting party that would take down two of the elk for the evening dinner. A few grabbed their hunting spears, and they split up. Five to the left flank and five to the right flank. This maneuver would undoubtedly land them a couple of elk. And off they went.

The elk stopped advancing and did not run or disperse when they saw the five groups moving in their direction but off to the sides. The elk just stood there and watched, and their heads turned left, then right, then left again, as they tried to keep an eye on the strangers in their land. All the time, they did not realize there was any danger or perhaps not fearing the stranger's advances.

Once the hunting group was in position, they gave the signal, and the hunters moved in quickly on the elk. Six of the hunters morphed into lions, and they bore down on the elks' positions. At this point, the elk realized their predicament, but two of them, one on the left and one on the right were not fast enough to escape the clutch of the attacking lions.

The first lion merely gored the elk's hind quarter and held tight, as a second lion locked his teeth into the thin part of his front right leg. The elk was immobilized as the third lion jumped onto his back, claws digging into the hide, and with a fully opened mouth, chewed into the side of its neck and held tight. The elk tried to fight, but the lions had it in a death grip, one they had successfully used in their many hunting trips over the years.

The first elk and the second elk went down, as the technique reflected the method used on the first elk. Once the elk was on the ground, the human-formed hunters moved in with the short spears to pierce the hearts and put the prey out of their misery.

The remaining elk had run from the attack, but they stopped not far away and watched the demise of their comrades. They saw their two friends, or family, killed before their eyes. It wasn't until the hunters looked up and in their direction that the remaining elk scampered away. They would not be following the villagers anymore.

The hunting group used their ropes to tie and drag the captured elk back to the bigger group. They would lose daylight soon, so they decided to camp and eat dinner. Everyone was excited to eat some freshly killed meat that wasn't a rabbit or squirrel like they had been eating over the past couple of weeks. They were also happy not to have to eat dried meat or dried fruit that they carried with them from the village when they left. Life on the move was not easy, and many felt getting out of their funk was a pleasant treat.

The Elders and some group leaders gathered off to the side to discuss the plan for the next day's movements. Since the forest they were in was uncharted to them, they had no real idea how far they would need to travel before coming out the other side. This made planning difficult but concise. The group would continue in a southerly direction until they exited the tree line. Until that time, proper planning could not be done.

"One other thing," GG Pa said, "something was very strange about those elk, and we should remain on high alert in case the others return."

The others agreed, and the watchers for the night were assigned. Three shifts, six per shift, and everyone must retain lion form during their watch. This would give them better night vision to identify any threats from afar.

***

At first light, the group leaders were already in place, and they were prodding the people to get their packs and be prepared to move out, even before a morning meal.

Sometime during the night, the weird-acting elk had left the area and were no longer eyeballing them from afar. The leaders thought this would be a great chance to move away from the area as soon as possible. They hoped that if the elk didn't see them when and if they came back, maybe the elk would go away and leave them alone.

It didn't take long for everyone to load up and start moving out. No one wanted to stay in the area longer than they had to. More importantly, there was still a lot of forest to cover, at least from what they could see. Not that they had any idea how far they still needed to go, but they knew they had to get away from where they were.

Maneek was the first elder to notice the bird in the tree ahead. It was a somewhat large bird. An eagle or a hawk, but it was a little large for even one of those birds. It was just sitting on one of the thicker branches of the tree, a short distance off to the left. Maneek tapped Tomas on the shoulder and pointed out the bird. This was the first bird they had seen since leaving the village. Birds were not plentiful in the region.

Tomas whispered to GG Pa and pointed towards the bird. GG Pa acknowledged but kept on walking. After a few more yards, he stepped out of the line and told the group, "We need to pick up the pace just a little more." The group started walking a bit faster, but GG Pa stayed in the same spot as they went by.

Once the last of the group passed him, GG Pa made a beeline for the bird on the branch. The bird sat still, looking at GG Pa until he was only feet away. Then, the bird dropped out of the tree and morphed into a human as he did. He nodded to GG Pa and said, "There is trouble brewing behind you. The elk are coming, and they are coming fast."

GG Pa asked, "How many are there, and should we be worried?"

The Hawkman said, "They are coming with their leader, the colossal elk. One of the 'Unintended,' and he is very angry at losing two of his children."

GG Pa asked, "How much time do we have?"

Hawkman replied, "One hour or a little more, but your group will be coming to a clearing soon, and that will make you vulnerable."

GG Pa turned and hurried to catch back up with his people as the man morphed back into a bird and flew away. Their quick meeting was over, and GG Pa now knew that an assailant was hot on their heels. He didn't want to scare the group but didn't want them to be unprepared when the elk caught up. He had to tell them and prepare for battle.

The Gate of M'Nayama

Nosoo had been camping out under this tree for a few weeks now. He spent his days hunting for food and learning the surrounding area while spending his nights watching for signs of the creatures and watching his back for predators. During the day, he knew there may be predators, but at least he could see them in the sunlight. At night, only the moon gave light, and it was not always available.

It was late in the day, and he thought about what he might be able to scrounge up for dinner. He thought about how much he missed the village and his family. How simple life was back there and the camaraderie of all the other villagers. The laughing, the playing, and the working were all parts of a full life he enjoyed as far back as he could remember. However, all that was gone now. The village and all the people were gone. Most of all, his self-respect was gone, all because of these creatures. He would find a way to bring them down.

He headed toward the lake, thinking he might catch a fish to eat. In his mind, he believed the lake might be haunted. It always felt eerie and strange whenever he was down there. One thing he told himself every time he went fishing, "Never go in deeper than your waist." Plus, he had no idea what the lake floor was like. It could have a sudden drop-off for which he was not ready. Staying safe in the water was important, even though he was putting his life on the line trying to even the score with an army of extra-large wolves.

When he arrived at the lake's edge, he saw a few ripples in the water, but he had no idea what could have caused them. They were not that big, so he thought a decent-sized fish might be in there. He hesitated for a few seconds to survey the area. Nothing different from when he came down to the lake to fish. He stepped into the water slowly because it was cold as usual, and he needed to ease into it.

Nosoo had spent many days alone in this wilderness, so he had a lot of time to think up stuff. He had thought about having the ability to morph only parts of his body into lion form, and he had been practicing this. He was already good at morphing limbs, as well as his head, without changing his torso.

He was going to use this new skill to improve his fishing.

He stood in the water, in human form, and morphed only his arms. He could morph his limbs, but it had to be both arms or legs. He could not do just one. He let a thin piece of root dangle in the water, looking enough like a worm to draw a fish. He stood perfectly still as he waited patiently for the unsuspecting fish.

It was a short time before a candidate for dinner swam up. The fish got just a hair too close as the lion's claw swept down on it and pierced its scaly flesh while scooping it out of the water. And just as the fish body and Nosoo's hand were coming out of the water, a long, dark presence swooped by so quickly that the pressure built up by the water knocked Nosoo off his feet and back towards the shore. He quickly and clumsily moved as fast as he could to get out of the water, but still holding tight to the fish he caught.

He fell backward, stumbling through the water and onto the dry land while still looking at the lake. "What the hell was that?" he thought. "I knew there was something funny about this lake."

He didn't get a good look at the presence that swept by, but he could discern that it was pretty long and very fast. Fishing in the lake was no longer an option for him. He would stick to sucking on rocks if he had to.

Nosoo took his prized fish back over to his "Eating Area." He had to have an eating area to avoid food remnants near or close to his shelter. He didn't want the smell or sight of the residue to lead to the discovery of his roost.

He had to dislodge the fish from his claw before morphing his arms back to human. He scaled the fish with his knife before cutting it open and removing the skeleton, almost whole. The fish's nice size made it much easier to remove the bones. The fish was a good fifteen pounds and three feet long. It was an excellent catch, but Nosoo felt that the fish was the bait, and he was supposed to be the catch.

**

After the hearty meal, Nosoo took a nap in his shelter. While he was napping, the sun went down, but the moon's light was bright. He rolled over, opened his eyes sleepily, and closed them again before his brain caught up. He quickly crawled out of his hideaway and looked up to the sky. The moon was almost full, and the sun was completely down. So why is it so bright?

He looked toward the mountain and saw the mysterious glow beginning to emanate right from the rock face. This was incredible. The rock was catching fire without flame, or heat. This was the source of the mystery glow he had seen from the village, but it was much more intense and unique up close. A slight humming sound also repeated its cadence every six or seven seconds.

Nosoo stood transfixed at the sight of the weird light coming from the side of the mountain until his mind returned to him, and he realized that it was probably not a good thing for him to stand there, in plain sight, watching. He quickly crawled back into his hideout and peered through the small openings. He tried to stay as still as possible so as not to draw any unwanted attention. The same way he did when he hid from the fight with the wolf army.

The glow lasted for hours, but just like the last time in the village, during the first night before the full moon, nothing happened. It was getting close to daybreak when the light's glow began to dim before fading entirely out. The anticipation died for Nosoo, but he knew there was a possibility that nothing would happen until the full moon. His problem was that he needed to track the actual day, even though he believed he had a good notion. When the glow began, he realized he had lost a few days somewhere.

Although the glow had stopped, Nosoo realized his search for the wolf army was about to end, making him sick. He had to talk himself down because his pulse ran three times the average speed. He could barely breathe. His nerves were shot, and his knees began to buckle. He hadn't seen any wolves yet, but he felt like one was standing on his chest.

His mind was racing at this point because he again realized that he had come all this way, determined and angry, but he didn't have a plan. He was flying by the seat of his pants to coin a phrase. He was one. They are an army. He is not tiny, but they are three times his size. He had witnessed how easily the wolves made short work of his lion family, and that was when fifty of them fought together.

"What the hell am I doing here?" he yelled into the openness.

Once he had calmed down, he realized it might serve him well to have something to eat, and it would not be fish from the lake. He had no intention of going back to the lake. He was setting his comfort zone at twenty feet from the edge of the lake, no closer. Whatever was in the lake needed to be avoided at all costs.

He would walk further into the forest for breakfast and gather some fruits. This was a much safer means of obtaining food and staying alive. There were things in the forest that could hurt you or kill you, but probably not as swift as what was lurking in the water.

Nosoo gathered several good fruits and nuts and returned them to his dining area. He ate slowly as he did some heavy thinking. Returning to the village was a non-starter since he knew all the people had left. Even if he left now and headed toward the kingdom, he had nothing to show for his actions, and the moniker of coward would be his to wear until his demise.

It was settled, he had to stay there and see this through. He would have to find the exact location of the wolf lair and bring the information to the king, along with whatever additional information he could gather about the wolves. To do that, he would have to suck it up and find some courage, do whatever must be done, and try not to get killed. So, he finished his breakfast and started to think.

***

The day went by fast. Nosoo occupied his time staking out the mountain in the area of the glow, which included running his hands along the rock face to try to understand the light. "Was there something about this part of the cliff that was different than the rock in the area that didn't glow? " He asked himself before feeling the cliff rock a little further to the left.

If there was a difference, he couldn't tell. Both areas felt identical. He was not a geologist. A rock is a rock, in his mind.

The sun would be going down soon, and he hadn't eaten his evening meal. He returned to his dining area and had more fruits and nuts from breakfast before returning to his hidden shelter.

The sun was now entirely down, and the moon was the only light in the sky when the rockface began illuminating. It started as if someone was slowly pushing up a dimmer switch from off. The increase in the illumination lasted over a period that must have been five minutes before it reached a peak. On this second night, the light from the rock was brighter than the evening before. Nosoo found it hard to look right at the glow once it peaked.

Unfortunately, or maybe it was, fortunately, nothing more happened that night. As the sun came up, Nosoo laid down and got some sleep.

***

When Nosoo awakened, he quickly looked around to ensure nothing had happened while he was asleep. Everything looked the same. Nothing stuck out as being different, so he crawled out of his hideout.

Once again, he felt hungry, so he went off to find food. He wanted to sink his teeth into something rather than eat fruits and nuts, but he knew the lake was a non-starter. He could venture further into the forest to see what he might find, but there were no guarantees. He decided to stick with the fruits and nuts.

It wasn't long before he saw that dusk was upon him, and the moon was in the sky. The sun wasn't entirely down, but the moon was high, and the rock began to hum. It was the hum of a vibration. Then came the glow. Very faint in the light of the still hovering sun, but a glow, nonetheless.

Nosoo moved quickly to his hiding spot and kept an eye on the mountain's vibrating and glowing rock face. Just as it had done previously, the glow intensified very slowly over the next hour or so, but as soon as the sun was out of sight, an opening began from the middle of the glow. It looked more like a Black Hole from space, opening to swallow a planet. The hole grew to the size of the light and more until it became a twenty-foot-high cavity. What started as a hole was now an opening to a cave.

Nosoo watched in amazement. He was tempted to look inside but held his ground in his hideout just in case the show wasn't over. Sure enough, the ground shook just a minute after the hole opened, and a rumbling sound came from the cave. The wolf army came jogging out of the cave, and there were more of them than he remembered from the fight in the field, but then again, he was hiding with his head down at the time. He had to put a hand over his mouth to ensure he didn't do anything to give away his position. In his mind, he was screaming, "Oh Crap, what the hell is this?"

This was an army. A large army. They were pouring out of the opening two at a time and jogging in cadence. They were on a mission, from what he could tell. Interestingly, they ran around the lake, and none of them went through it. They were headed back in the same direction as before. In the same way, he had followed their tracks from the field where his friends were killed. Where could they possibly be going?

Once the last of the group was out of sight, Nosoo carefully slipped out of his hiding place and morphed into his lion form. He slowly crept closer toward the cave opening, keeping low and alert. His head was on a swivel as he looked at the cave and then the lake, in case one of them (or all of them) were coming back.

He reached the cave opening and cautiously peeked inside. One eye first, then slowly moving to allow his entire face to look inside.

Looking inside, there was nothing special about the cave besides the glow surrounding the outside; the entrance was just a dark, dank, run-of-the-mill cave entrance.

Keeping low to the ground and close to the wall, Nosoo crawled inside the cave. A light was coming from the left, deeper into the cave, so he made his way in that direction, still keeping low and moving slowly and keeping his head on the swivel until he reached the area from where the light was coming. Now he saw that this was not just some ordinary cave. This place was like nothing he had ever seen.

Encounter the Elk

GG Pa caught up with the back of the group before signaling the leaders to bring the march to a halt.

The group stopped five hundred feet from the clearing, where the tree line would end. Everyone was surprised they were stopping when they knew that those weird elk were coming for them. So, plenty of murmurs were going through the crowd before GG Pa made it to the front to address the group. It took a minute to get the people to be quiet to communicate the information.

Once they had calmed down, GG Pa told them that the elk were still coming from behind, but now they were joined by a giant elk who was very angry. Running, or attempting to flee, was no longer an option because the giant elk ran much faster than they could. The best option is to stand and fight, and it cannot be in the open field because the elk would have the upper hand. Staying in the forest would benefit the villagers because the trees hamper the giant elk's ability to fight. Also, we will fight in human form, with hand spears and machetes.

Shujaa, the Elder, yelled, "All adults, spread out and position yourselves close to the trees. Use the trees as shields. Youngsters and children are to move closer to the clearing but do not go into the open field. Stay close to the trees and keep the trees between you and the elk."

The large group split up into several smaller groups, and the younger villagers moved toward the end of the tree line without going into the clearing. The younger people were also tasked with bringing the many backpacks closer to the end of the tree line so that the packs wouldn't be in the way. The adults gathered two and three to a group behind the trees and spread over a reasonable span of ground in a 'U' shape. This way, by the time the elk saw the people in front of them, there would already be others coming up from behind.

The group was in position just in time before the elk showed up, and sure enough, there was a giant elk with them. The giant elk stood about fifteen feet high without the antlers. You could hear grunts as he breathed when he walked and there was a slight vibration in the earth when this thing's hoofs hit the ground as it galloped.

The giant was the main problem, so the villagers knew not to waste time on the regular-sized elk. Bringing down the giant was the main objective, so just as the giant was passing the middle of their fight line, the villagers behind those trees jumped out and hit the giant's legs with their machetes, causing some deep gashes, but the giant continued forward.

At the next set of trees, the villagers jumped out and stabbed the giant with several spears, also in the legs. This had an effect. The giant slowed in its movement and then stopped. It let out a loud and excruciating roar. So loud that the smaller elk seemed to freeze, just for a second, before turning directly to the group of villagers that had just stabbed the giant. The elk charged at them, full throttle. Using the trees as shields, they all safely side-stepped the elk attack.

Now, all the villagers charged at the giant with machetes and spears. They began stabbing and slashing at every part of his body that they could reach. Blood spurted and squirted because the villagers knew how much of a life-and-death situation this was. One villager did get gored by an elk when he didn't expect it.

Another villager was brushed by an elk's antlers, causing a bruise, but he escaped any considerable damage by moving just in time. A third villager took an elk antler straight in his chest, driving him into a tree. He did not survive. The fight was brutal, even after neutralizing the most significant threat, the giant. He was down but not entirely out. By taking out his legs, the danger he posed was cut down by eighty percent. The villagers just had to stay away from his mouth and antlers.

One of the regular-sized elk moved toward the group of youngsters near the end of the tree line. He was running fast towards the group, and this spooked a couple of the younger villagers. When the first one ran, the second one did, too, from reflex. The two of them ran out into the clearing as fast as they could. Even morphing into lions did not help much, as the large elk on their tail was an adult, and it was swift. The elk was gaining ground on the two very fast. It was not looking good for them. Someone was going to get hurt.

The shadow overhead appeared suddenly, and just as quickly, two large falcons swooped down and scooped up the young lions in their talons. It carried them up and out of the reach of the charging elk, then made an arching semi-circle high above the grassy field before flying them back to the tree line, near their safe position before the chase began. The falcons descended to ten feet above the ground, dropped the young lions there, and flew off.

Having seen the large elk chasing the young lions, several adult lions were already moving in on the elk. Contrary to their usual hunting approach, these lions pounce directly on the elk, claws, and teeth presented. With no time to react, the elk went down quickly and was ripped to shreds. This kill was for the lives of their offspring, not for sport or food. Once this elk was done, the lions returned to the primary fight in the forest area and ran back to help the rest of the group.

The fight was almost over. The one thing that would end it was for the lions to kill the giant elk.

Several lions came up from behind and ran straight up on his back. He was limited in his movement, so he was helpless to stop them. Strategically, they began to attack his spine in different areas. Ripping and tearing through his thick fur and tough skin. The giant elk let out a scream that shook the forest and froze the other elk in their tracks, but the lions didn't stop.

More lions were stabbing the giant elk's torso, like 'The Death of a Thousand Cuts,' and he was bleeding profusely. His demise was at hand.

Those elk who had survived the fight and could move on their own ran back into the forest.

The giant elk's chin hit the ground as his eyes dimmed and shut. All movement stopped, even the lions. No one moved. The fight was over. The villagers had won.

***

Many villagers ran to help the wounded, while others ran to check on the young ones. Lions were morphing into human forms and reuniting with their families and friends. There were a few smiles, but those were smiles of relief along with tears of exasperation.

Two of the lions had been wounded. One was a mere abrasion that would hurt for a few days, but it would heal in a matter of time. The other was a gash, which was a bit more and required bandages and other medicines. This kind of wound is susceptible to infection, so keeping it clean would be paramount. They were not in a position, out in the wilderness, to treat the wound how it needed to be treated, so getting to the kingdom for more help was their best bet.

There was also one fatality, and that was Boone. He was a good protector and a wonderful father. He wanted to go with the fighters who fought with the wolves, but he was selected to stay and help protect the village that day. Since then, he has given his all to defend his family and the villagers from all perceived dangers. To him, it was an honor to die for his people.

Unfortunately, there was no time for funerals or honoraria today. The group had to use this opportunity to put as much distance between them and this place. The last thing they needed was for the elk to return with reinforcements or even another giant elk.

The leaders got the group back together and ready to move out. Some elk were hacked up, and the meat was distributed for transport. Two villagers banded together to help assist the wounded, while four others made it their responsibility to carry the body of Boone until they could have a funeral.

Once they had it all together, the villagers moved out and across the open field. They had cleared the forest and were progressing toward the kingdom again.

***

The day had turned to late afternoon before the travelers felt safe enough to stop. This was a place to rest, snack, and bury Boone. Nothing more.

Boone was laid to rest in a somber ceremony, lacking the usual traditions. There would be no markings on his grave. Hoping this would prevent any beast, or anything, from identifying and desecrating it. His honor would be where it mattered most in their hearts and minds. His family would still be proud of his sacrifice.

They changed the bandages on the wounded, had a small meal, and began moving again. This time, they would keep moving until dusk before stopping and camping.

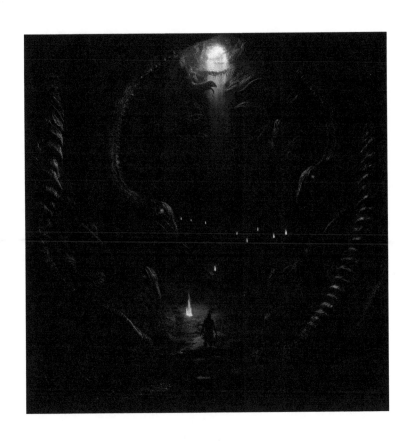

Here They Come

The cave passage opened into an enormous salon of the eerie. The ceiling rose to fifty or sixty feet, with a large opening at the top, similar to a skylight.

The cave walls were adorned with incredible carved figures and busts of weirdly beaked snake-like creatures with prickly spines and glowing red eyes. They were of many sizes and ran to the top, stopping just short of the opening in the ceiling. Nothing moved, and there was no sound other than the crackle of the small fires that adorned the walkway through the cave.

Nosoo was so consumed with the unbelievable stature of the cave that he was not fully aware of how far into the cave he had walked. He had strolled halfway through the salon area before he stopped to look back and regain his senses. If he had not fully committed to investigating the cave, he realized it may be too late to turn around now. Also, based on the time it took the wolf army to return after the fight in the fields, he guessed that he still had plenty of time to look around some more before returning to the cave opening.

Now, he walked quicker along the lighted path but continued to watch his back and both sides. He passed some of the weirdest-looking wall carvings, and a few seemed to be expanding and contracting almost as if they were breathing. Even the cave floor, along the sides of the path, looked to be moving a little. He almost slithered along as he walked, but his attention was diverted as he reached another dark passage similar to the cave entrance.

He slowed his pace once more before peering around the bend. One eye first so as not to be seen, in case someone, or something, was around the corner. When the coast seemed clear, he let his entire head lean out to look ahead, down the passageway. There was nothing there, just darkness with a dull light at the end, which looked like the cave's mouth. Now, it was time to get down low again and cautiously move.

After creeping slowly to the mouth of the cave, he glanced around outside and saw an entirely different world, or so it seemed. Everything was in darkness. There were trees with no leaves, and they were twisted in horrible shapes as if they were in constant pain. There was no grass, but there were barren hedges in sporadic places. And there were plenty of rocks of all sizes for as far as the eye could see.

It was quiet and spooky, even more than the inside of the cave. Nothing here was moving, and the little light was reflected from a more significant light, far off in the distance. He thought there may be others at the light source, and he was no match for these things, so it was time to go.

Just as he turned to go back into the cave, the ground began to shake.

"Oh no. They're back," he said aloud.

Just then, something flying in the distance let out a loud shriek. Nosoo might have crapped his pants if he had some on. Instead, he eyed a considerable boulder off to his left and made a mad dash for it. He was running as fast as his lion legs would take him. He ran behind it and crouched real low in the dark as he peered out toward the mouth of the cave. The ground was rumbling something awful now, and it was just seconds before the first wolf creature emerged from the cave. He was followed by what seemed to be an endless line of wolf creatures. Nosoo was too frightened to even think about counting them.

Once the last creature had passed his sightline and it looked like the coast was clear, Nosoo dashed for the cave entrance and the safety, he believed it held. He quickly slinked out of sight but checked his back to ensure he wasn't spotted. The coast was clear, so he traced his path back through the cave, but when he turned the corner toward the large, cavernous opening, he stopped hard in his tracks, and the nervous shiver was uncontrollable as he observed the large cave carvings were not carvings at all. They were alive, moving, and they may have seen him.

Immediately, Nosoo ran back the other way out of the cave and into the darkness of this weird place and back to the large boulder that offered him cover from the wolves.

Breathing hard and shaking like a leaf, he realized quickly he was trapped in this mysterious world.

END NOTES

Don't miss Volume Two:

The villagers arrive at the kingdom of Imbube.

The mysterious world of M'Nayama.

More human hybrids are unveiled.

And the story of the 'Unintended' will be told.

9 798869 097385